W9-BAB-869

This has to be a nightmare. It's the only possible explanation, Jessica thought. A few minutes earlier, Jessica and her twin sister, Elizabeth, had heard footsteps enter the cabin behind them. They had spun around, expecting to see their mother.

The next few seconds had played out in slow motion. Jessica remembered seeing a glass of water fall from her sister's hand to the table near the bunk beds. She remembered water splashing her own bare thighs, near the hem of her cutoffs. And she remembered recoiling in horror at the sight of John Marin standing over them, his hair damp and disheveled, a straight, sharp knife glittering in his hand.

Now Marin held that same knife, cold against the front of Jessica's throat.

Two weeks earlier, she would have snuggled deliciously into the powerful arm that was wrapped around her bare midriff. But now its pressure on her skin made her feel dirty.

"How did you get here?" she sobbed. "How did you follow us?"

Marin laughed. "Shut up, darling," he sneered. "And do exactly as I tell you."

A KILLER
ON BOARD

Written by
Kate William

Created by
FRANCINE PASCAL

BANTAM BOOKS
NEW YORK · TORONTO · LONDON · SYDNEY · AUCKLAND

RL 6, age 12 and up

A KILLER ON BOARD

A Bantam Book / August 1995

Sweet Valley High® is a registered trademark of Francine Pascal
Conceived by Francine Pascal
Produced by Daniel Weiss Associates, Inc.
33 West 17th Street
New York, NY 10011
Cover art by Bruce Emmett

All rights reserved.
Copyright © 1995 by Francine Pascal.
Cover art copyright © 1995 by Daniel Weiss Associates, Inc.
No part of this book may be reproduced or transmitted
in any form or by any means, electronic or mechanical,
including photocopying, recording, or by any information
storage and retrieval system, without permission in
writing from the publisher.
For information address: Bantam Books

If you purchased this book without a cover you should be aware
that this book is stolen property. It was reported as "unsold and
destroyed" to the publisher and neither the author nor the publisher
has received any payment for this "stripped book."

ISBN: 0-553-56714-4

Published simultaneously in the United States and Canada

Bantam Books are published by Bantam Books, a division of Bantam Doubleday Dell Publishing Group, Inc. Its trademark, consisting of the words "Bantam Books" and the portrayal of a rooster, is Registered in U.S. Patent and Trademark Office and in other countries. Marca Registrada. Bantam Books, 1540 Broadway, New York, New York 10036.

PRINTED IN THE UNITED STATES OF AMERICA

OPM   0 9 8 7 6 5 4 3 2 1

To John Stewart Carmen

Chapter 1

A hand tightened on Elizabeth Wakefield's shoulder. She gasped. The silverware she'd been holding clattered to the dining-room table. Elizabeth whirled around, expecting to see the handsome, cruel face and the glittering midnight-blue eyes that had haunted her dreams for days.

Instead she found her identical twin, Jessica, staring at her with startled blue-green eyes. "Oh, Liz," Jessica began. "I'm sorry I scared you. You must've thought . . . I mean . . ."

Elizabeth sighed, knowing her own eyes had the same unsettled look as her sister's. "It's all right, Jessica. I guess we're all jumpy after what happened Saturday night."

"Can you blame us?" Jessica asked. "That creep would've murdered us if Dad hadn't—" She swallowed. "Anyhow, sixteen is definitely too young to die."

1

Elizabeth shuddered. "I don't want to talk about Saturday night, or last week, or John Marin. I wish I could forget he ever existed."

"Me, too," Jessica declared. "And usually I'm so good at forgetting things!" She tossed her sister a handful of napkins.

With only a small flicker of a smile, Elizabeth caught the napkins and began folding them in triangles by the sides of the dinner plates. Under normal circumstances she would have been grateful for her sister's company. Usually nobody was better at cheering her up than Jessica. But right now even her entertaining twin couldn't take Elizabeth's mind off last Saturday night.

Elizabeth stared at a butter knife that lay on the table in front of her. She remembered the starlit sky above the Pacific Ocean, off the coast of their southern-California town. For the first hour of her date on Saturday, she'd been in heaven. It had been a breezy, romantic night, and she had danced on the deck of a sailing yacht with a young man she had found exciting and glamorous—a man whose name was supposed to be Ben.

Then the night had crashed down around her like a cold ocean wave. Elizabeth remembered the wind ripping at her long blond hair and the sailboat's deck lurching under her feet. Nearly blinded by the searing searchlights of the nearby coast-guard cutter, Elizabeth had struggled desperately with Marin as he'd tried to stab her with his gleaming knife.

The knife on the dining-room table flashed as Jessica slid it into place in front of their mother's chair. Elizabeth jumped.

"Liz?"

"Oh, I'm sorry, Jess. I guess I was spacing out."

Jessica stared at her. "I know. I've been doing the same thing all week. I'll be talking to Mom, or listening to a CD, and all of a sudden—wham!— I'm back in the storage room at the cafe, seeing John Marin's shadow on the wall as he tries to stab me." She shuddered visibly. "I think it's contagious. Mom and Dad seem spooked, too."

Elizabeth nodded her head in agreement. "It must be really hard on Mom. Can you imagine coming home from a business trip and finding out that your daughters and your husband were nearly murdered while you were gone?"

Jessica bit her lip. "I sure wish *I* had been away on a business trip Saturday night."

"I'm glad you weren't," Elizabeth told her, her voice softening. "You saved my life, Jess. If you hadn't been around to jump into the water when I hit my head—"

Jessica shook her head. "Don't, Liz. I don't want to think about it."

"Neither do I, but the images keep coming back."

Jessica sighed. "For me, too. This afternoon Prince Albert brushed up against me in the kitchen, and I actually screamed—as if Marin

3

would come waltzing into our kitchen disguised as a golden retriever."

"I wouldn't put it past him, if he ever got paroled again," Elizabeth said. "He managed to fool both of us about his real identity for a whole week. I can't believe he had me convinced he was a novelist and a sailor."

Jessica momentarily covered her eyes with her hands. "That's nothing," she sighed. "I actually thought he worked for a television producer. I halfway believed I was falling in love with that degenerate."

"So did I," Elizabeth added softly.

Jessica took a deep breath and managed a smile. "Well, we're safe now. Marin's back in prison, waiting for his trial. At least they didn't let him out on bail."

"Not with all those parole violations," Elizabeth said. "Besides, the charges are too serious. It's two counts of murder—"

"For killing those poor men Dad hired to protect us—"

"Along with all the other charges," Elizabeth continued with a shudder, "for the things he tried to do to us."

Jessica faced her twin and her eyes flashed. "I'm sure he'll get convicted of everything. So don't be afraid, Lizzie. John Marin can't hurt us anymore."

❖　　❖　　❖

4

A half hour later Jessica let her fork fall to her plate with a loud clink. "That's it, Dad!" she said in an exasperated voice. "I can't take another second of this."

Her father's brown eyes widened with a look of fake innocence. "Whatever do you mean?"

"You've been smiling like a jack-o'-lantern from the moment you walked in the front door," Jessica told her father. "What's the big secret?"

Mr. Wakefield grinned more broadly. "I was going to wait to spring it on you over dessert."

"Spill it, Dad," Jessica urged. "Secrets were meant to be blabbed."

"Spoken by one who knows," Elizabeth said with a smirk. Jessica threw her a dirty look.

"I'm with Jessica this time," Mrs. Wakefield said. "We could all use some good news, Ned."

"OK, OK! You've beaten it out of me." He sat back in his chair and smiled at his family. "How would you all like to go on a little vacation?"

"Where—" Jessica began.

"I don't know, Ned," Mrs. Wakefield said, interrupting her daughter. "I'm right in the middle of my remodeling job." The twins' mother ran a successful interior-design firm in the Wakefields' hometown of Sweet Valley, California.

"Can't you take a little time off, Alice? The mansion in Bridgewater will still be there next week," her husband said. "Let the architect handle things without you for a few days. Besides, didn't you suggest just a week ago that we get out of town for a little while?"

Jessica opened her mouth again, but her mother spoke before she had the chance to make a sound.

"Yes, I suppose I did," Mrs. Wakefield said wistfully. "And it sounds tempting. After last week, we do need to spend some time together as a family."

"Some time *where*—?" Jessica asked.

"What about Steven?" Elizabeth asked at the same time. "Will he be able to get back from Sacramento to come with us?" The twins' eighteen-year-old brother was a summer intern with his father's law firm. Mr. Wakefield had sent him to the state capital for a few weeks to help an attorney who was working with a legislative subcommittee.

"No, I already called Steven," Mr. Wakefield said. "I sent him to Sacramento to keep him safe from Marin, but he's been so much help to Amanda that I doubt she'll want to let him go."

"*Go where?*" Jessica practically screamed. "In case you hadn't noticed, I'm dying of curiosity here—"

"Oh, Ned," Mrs. Wakefield interrupted. "Surely, Amanda would—"

"Of course she would let him take a week off if I asked her to," Mr. Wakefield said. "But Steven doesn't want to leave, as long as we're all safe and sound. He says he's learned more in the last two weeks than he did in his entire first year of prelaw classes."

6

Jessica grabbed a bowl of salsa and stood up. "Is someone going to tell me exactly where we're going?" she demanded. "If I don't find out within the next minute, I swear I'll drink this entire bowl of extra-hot salsa right here and now—and then you'll all have to watch me writhing on the floor in agony!"

Her father laughed. "I was thinking of an island vacation—"

"Hawaii!" Jessica shrieked, almost upsetting the bowl of salsa. "We're going to Hawaii! Wait till I tell Lila!" For once she would have a vacation that could compete with her wealthy best friend Lila Fowler's exotic trips. "I'll need a new bikini, and—"

Her father took her arm and gently pulled her back into her seat. "Jessica, slow down. Hawaii isn't exactly what I had in mind. But how about a week on Catalina Island?"

"That's not as good as Hawaii," Jessica admitted. "But it's a whole lot better than a week here!"

Her mother smiled. "It sounds wonderful, honey."

"What about work?" Elizabeth asked. "Jessica and I started waitressing less than two weeks ago. I don't know if Mr. Jenkins will be able to find replacements on such short notice."

Leave it to Liz to bring up work, Jessica thought. "Don't worry about it," she told her sister. "Jane and the other waitresses are desperate for more tips. They would love the extra shifts!"

"Are you sure?" Mr. Wakefield asked. "I could call Mr. Jenkins in the morning and talk to him myself."

"Well, Mr. Jenkins has been awfully nice to us, after what happened last weekend," Elizabeth said. "He said to take off some time if we thought we needed to—although I think he meant only a day or two."

"It's not a problem," Jessica said, waving her hand. "He probably feels guilty that Marin tried to attack me in his restaurant. He'll let us take as long as we want."

"I know!" Elizabeth said, snapping her fingers. "Maria Santelli said she wanted to earn some money for her cousin's wedding present. She'd jump at the chance to take on a few shifts at the Marina Cafe."

Jessica snorted. "Especially since Winston Egbert, Mr. Geek, is working at the beach nearby. It's sickening, the way those two are all over each other."

"I think it's sweet," Elizabeth said. "They make a nice couple."

"What's Winston doing at the beach this summer?" Mr. Wakefield asked, an amused look on his face. Like the twins, Winston was a junior at Sweet Valley High, and even the adults in town knew of his reputation for being the class clown.

"Winston is in charge of beach maintenance," Jessica said. "That means he's the beach *janitor*. Can you think of anything more gross than cleaning up after people?"

"It's no worse than being a waitress," Elizabeth reminded her. "Besides, Winston says he's a 'coastal-enhancement engineer.'"

Jessica rolled her eyes. "He would."

Elizabeth sighed. "Anyway, Maria is very responsible. And she has waitressing experience. I'll call her tonight. I think Mr. Jenkins will go along with the idea."

"Whatever," Jessica said. "So when do we leave?"

"I have us penciled in for two rooms at the Hotel Orizaba, beginning Saturday night," the girls' father told them. "We'll drive down to San Pedro the day after tomorrow and take the channel boat to Catalina."

"Cool!" Jessica said. "The Orizaba is supposed to be one of the ritziest resorts on the island. That'll show Lila!"

"How in the world did you manage rooms at the Orizaba, Ned?" Mrs. Wakefield asked. "Or anywhere on Catalina? I thought every room on the island was booked solid every summer, months in advance."

Her husband shrugged. "One of the partners in my firm—you know Marianna West—was supposed to go on vacation next week. But the

9

depositions in the West Coast Oilcam case were pushed back. I know you've all heard me talking about the Oilcam case. It's a wrongful-dismissal action—"

"This is all very exciting, Dad," Jessica interrupted, rolling her eyes. "But is there a point to this story?"

"The point is that Oilcam is Marianna's case," Mr. Wakefield explained patiently, "so she's stuck with the extra work. She'll be at the office all weekend, in fact."

"I thought you were working on that case with Marianna," Elizabeth pointed out. "Won't you be tied up all weekend, too?"

"Not anymore. We decided today that it would be good experience for Griffin Pierce to take over for me." Mr. Wakefield smiled gleefully. Jessica remembered that Griffin Pierce was a money-grubbing young associate that her father couldn't stand. "Anyway," he continued, "it means that Marianna has to give up her reservations for two rooms for all next week—"

"I always liked her!" Jessica interrupted, grinning.

"We certainly could use some relaxation," Mrs. Wakefield added. "Ever since I got back into town Sunday, I've been so skittish that I jump every time the phone rings. I don't think I slept at all last night."

Her husband put his arm around her shoulders.

"You're not the only one," he said, glancing at the twins. The whole family, Jessica realized, looked worn and haggard. Mr. Wakefield sighed. "It'll be nice to leave our troubles behind for a week of nothing but pure relaxation."

Chapter 2

Later that night Elizabeth leaned her elbow on her desk, cradling the telephone against her ear. She heard a door creak open behind her. "Get out, Jessica!" she called without turning around. Only one person ever came through the door that led to the bathroom between her room and her sister's. "Can't you see I'm on the phone?"

"I'll wait," Jessica said, punctuating her words with a snap of bubblegum. Bedsprings squeaked as she made herself comfortable.

Elizabeth whirled in her seat to glare at her twin, who was sitting cross-legged on the neatly made bed, spreading some papers in front of her on the comforter. Elizabeth turned back to the desk. Ignoring Jessica was always easier than trying to get rid of her. "I'm sorry, Todd," she said into the receiver. "It's only Jessica."

13

Elizabeth's longtime boyfriend, Todd Wilkins, had never been one of Jessica's biggest fans, but now he laughed. "As usual," he said. "Well, for once I'm not going to complain about Jessica popping in unexpectedly. I owe her one, since she saved your life last weekend."

"And I owe *you* one. I'm sorry I acted like such a jerk all last week," Elizabeth said softly, apologizing for the fourth time since Sunday morning. She could feel her sister's gossip radar tuned in on the conversation, and she was glad that Jessica could hear only one side of it.

"Liz, you have nothing to apologize for," Todd said. "*I* was the jerk—for not realizing how bored you were."

"No, Todd—"

"Yes, Liz. You were right. We've been in a rut. If I hadn't been so oblivious, we could have worked it out together. Then you wouldn't have thought you had to sneak around with Ben, or Marin, or whatever the guy's real name is."

Elizabeth shook her head. "But it was wrong of me to see someone else," she admitted. "I knew it, and I did it anyway."

"I won't argue with you there. And if you hadn't nearly got yourself killed, I'd probably be furious. As it is, I'm just glad you're all right." He lowered his voice, and Elizabeth sensed anger beneath his words. "But if you ever date somebody else behind my back again . . ."

14

"Don't worry!" she assured him. "I've learned my lesson. And I've had enough excitement these last few weeks to last for a year. As soon as I return from Catalina, I'm looking forward to going back to our happy little rut!"

"Have a great week, Liz," Todd said tenderly. "And remember that I love you."

With a pleasant warmth in her chest, Elizabeth slowly hung up the phone, thinking about Todd's deep-brown eyes and soft, wavy hair. It was hard to believe that she'd been dissatisfied with him only a week earlier.

"How's lover boy?" Jessica asked.

Elizabeth turned to see her blowing an enormous pink bubble. "Haven't you ever heard of a private conversation?"

Jessica deflated the bubble with her tongue. After she'd loudly sucked the gum back into her mouth, she said, "Private? But we're identical twins. We share everything, remember?"

"Right. The way we share *my* sweaters, *my* jeans, *my* blouses . . ."

Jessica shrugged. "That's a nice way to talk to someone who saved your life."

"I already thanked you for that!" Elizabeth objected, annoyed.

"You know, the whole coast guard may have been there Saturday night, but I was the only one who was watching you instead of Marin," Jessica reminded her.

15

"Don't change the subject!" Elizabeth broke in. "We were talking about your interrupting me. Todd and I were having a private conversation."

"What's the big deal? It was pretty tame, if you ask me."

"OK, OK," Elizabeth said with a sigh. Sometimes arguing with Jessica just wasn't worth the trouble. "Let's drop it. So what's up? I assume you came in here for something besides eavesdropping on my phone calls."

"What did Maria say?" Jessica asked. "I didn't start eavesdropping soon enough to hear that call."

"She said she'd love to be a waitress for a week. I'll speak to Mr. Jenkins in the morning, and she'll have an interview with him tomorrow afternoon about taking some of our shifts."

"Great!" Jessica said. "We definitely got the best of that deal. Catalina's going to be fantastic!" She waved a handful of glossy pamphlets.

"What are those?"

"Brochures about the island and the Hotel Orizaba," Jessica replied. "Dad said we should read through them and get an idea of all the fun things we want to do next week."

"I'd be happy just sitting on a nice, warm, safe beach, reading a mystery novel."

"Bor-ing!" Jessica pronounced. "Are you sure you're my sister? Sometimes I think you were abducted by aliens as an infant and replaced with an Elizabeth look-alike."

16

"Boring is exactly what I'm looking for," Elizabeth said. "Don't you think we've had enough adventure for one summer?"

"Nah," Jessica said. "Just the wrong kind of adventure. Sitting on the beach is OK, but reading books is definitely out. School ended two weeks ago! Beaches aren't for reading, anyway. They're for showing off in a bikini, working on your tan, and scoping out good-looking surfers."

"What about Ken?" Elizabeth asked. In the last few months Jessica had begun seriously dating Ken Matthews, the star quarterback for the Sweet Valley High Gladiators.

"If Ken were on the beach in Catalina, I'd scope him out, too," Jessica said diplomatically. "But he's still on vacation with his parents. So what's wrong with looking at other guys?"

"Isn't that what got you into trouble last week?" Elizabeth asked.

"*Looking* at cute guys never got anyone in trouble." Jessica smiled at her sister. "It's all that stuff you do *after* you look that can be a problem."

Elizabeth folded her arms. "Since when do you stop at just looking?"

"Don't worry," Jessica said. "After what happened with Scott—I mean *Marin*—I plan to restrict myself to just looking for a while."

"I'm sure that dozens of surfers on Catalina will be sorry to hear that."

"But really, Liz, we're perfectly safe now. The

17

odds of running into *another* super-sexy guy who's also a serial killer are practically nonexistent. There just aren't that many murderers out there, and we already found one this summer. So, statistically, there's no danger anymore."

Elizabeth laughed. "I can't argue with logic like that."

"Of course not," Jessica said. She snapped her gum. "Remember, I took statistics last year."

"And got a C-minus, I seem to recall."

"Oh, *grades* are no big deal," Jessica said, waving the whole concept away with her hand. Studying had never been high on her priority list.

"I'll keep that in mind," Elizabeth said, thinking of her own straight-A report card. "So what's in these brochures? Tips on the best beaches for watching surfers?"

"Yep. That's in this one," Jessica said, pointing to a pamphlet. On the cover a blond man and woman stood on a sandy beach, silhouetted against an orange sunset. Jessica fanned out the other brochures. "There's also stuff on shopping, snorkeling, and tennis. We're going to have the best time, Liz."

"This does look like fun," Elizabeth agreed, scanning another brochure. "Listen to this, Jess. It says here that visitors aren't allowed to drive cars on the island. Everyone gets around by walking, taking the shuttle bus, or renting golf carts."

"Lame!" Jessica announced. "It'll be difficult to look glamorous on a shuttle bus." She paged through another leaflet and then glanced up at her twin excitedly. "I've got it! We'll go horseback riding! It says here that the resort we're staying at has a ranch. We can rent horses and go on guided horseback rides."

"We haven't been horseback riding in ages," Elizabeth said.

"True," Jessica agreed, nodding her head. "But we used to be pretty good at it. And horseback riding is like riding a bicycle—you never forget. You know, I'm always amazed at just how good guys look on horseback."

"Jess, do you ever think about anything else?" Elizabeth asked.

"Not if I can help it," Jessica replied.

Elizabeth shook her head and pulled another brochure from the pile. Jessica was hopeless. "The botanical garden sounds beautiful," she tried. "And look at these pictures of the shoreline! Isn't this gorgeous?" She pointed to a photograph that showed an isolated cove surrounded by sheer bluffs.

"It says you can take a tour around the coastline of the island in a glass-bottom boat. That might be cool."

"No, thanks!" Elizabeth said. "As much as I love boats, I've had enough of them to last me a long, long time." She shuddered, her mind flashing back to her desperate struggle for Marin's knife on the deck of his sailboat. "Once we get to the island, I'm going to keep my feet on solid ground for the whole vacation!"

Chapter 3

Leighann LeShay adjusted the gun in her shoulder holster. Then she smoothed her frizzy black hair and took a deep breath. Thursday's night shift was about to start. "I hate this job," she told her reflection in the women's bathroom mirror.

"You aren't the only one, honey," said a short, round woman who emerged from a stall. "I've worked in this stinking prison for fourteen years. And believe me, those filthy-mouthed Neanderthals never let up for a minute." She pulled out a comb and ran it through her short gray-blond hair. "By the way, the name's Phyllis," she said, sticking out a hand.

"I'm Leighann. And you're right about the filthy language. In the last two weeks I've heard more four-letter words than I knew existed."

"I bet you have," the older woman said. "The

inmates must think you're real pretty. And you're young." She cocked her head. "How old are you? You don't look any more than eighteen."

Leighann stretched to her full height of five foot one. "I'm twenty-three."

Phyllis nodded. "Like I said, you're young. So these reptiles probably hassle you a heck of a lot worse than they hassle me. How long you been on the job, hon?"

"Exactly two weeks," Leighann said. "Cellblock A."

Phyllis laughed. "That says it all. Cellblock A always seems to have the worst, uh, *customers*. The cream of the scum, you know?"

"Tell me about it," Leighann said. "Is there any way to shut them up?"

"Not really," Phyllis replied. "But you've got to act like it doesn't bother you. They'll hassle you worse if they see that it's getting to you."

Leighann smoothed out the blouse of her guard's uniform. "But how can I pretend it doesn't bother me when they say nasty, disgusting things?"

"Just put on your best poker face when they start to get rowdy." Phyllis demonstrated her best uncaring expression in the mirror—her eyes closed halfway, and her mouth became a tight, hard line. "Then visualize yourself as John Wayne or Clint Eastwood. Cool and confident."

Leighann tried to copy Phyllis's expression, but she thought her eyes still looked too friendly and trusting. She grimaced. "I was always lousy at poker," she said with a sigh. Then Leighann turned away from the mirror and pushed open the bathroom door. "Well, it's time to enter the reptile house. See you around."

She moved slowly toward cellblock A, steeling herself for the catcalls and leers that always followed her as she walked the block. There were only a few female guards at the state prison, and most were much older than Leighann. When she was on duty, the prisoners vied with each other to come up with the raunchiest jeers. All except the prisoner in cell 202. He seemed to be a real gentleman.

Leighann passed through the metal detector and stopped at the steel-barred gate at the entrance to the cellblock. Again she straightened her blue-gray uniform. Then she pushed her way into cellblock A, hoping the polite, handsome young man in 202 would be awake.

Jessica sat in the driver's seat of the black Jeep the twins shared, drumming her fingers on the steering wheel. She and Elizabeth had just finished working Friday's lunch shift at the cafe, and she was eager to get home and start packing for the trip.

"Finally!" Jessica exclaimed as her twin opened the passenger-side door and climbed into the Jeep. "What took you so long? You said you were coming out right behind me."

"Sorry, Jess," Elizabeth said. "But Todd came in to say good-bye."

"We're spending a week on Catalina—not a year in Kathmandu," Jessica reminded her sister. "Can't you two get along without each other for seven measly days?"

"Of course we can," Elizabeth said with a grin. "But we haven't caught up yet from not seeing much of each other last week. Can you blame us for wanting to say good-bye?"

Jessica gunned the engine. "I swear, Liz, you were more interesting when you decided to add some excitement to your life."

"That kind of excitement I don't need," Elizabeth said. "And neither do you. Besides, don't you miss Ken at all?"

Jessica was about to open her mouth to say she didn't. But she shut it. She liked to think she was totally independent and didn't need any one guy to make her happy. But every time she thought of Ken's sun-bleached hair and broad shoulders, a wave of loneliness washed over her. "Yes," she admitted. "I guess I do miss him."

Elizabeth gave her a knowing look. "You say that as if you were confessing something awful. There's nothing wrong with liking somebody special. Ken's a great guy."

"I know. But I'm supposed to be Jessica love-'em-and-leave-'em Wakefield, the free agent. I can't believe I've actually got myself tied down."

24

Elizabeth stared at her curiously. "Are you saying you're not in love with Ken anymore?"

"That's just the problem," Jessica said. "I do love Ken! I'm happier when he's here. Isn't that a drag?"

"I see what you mean. Love and happiness—ugh!"

"I thought there was some hope for you last week," Jessica said. "But I was wrong. You're as boring as ever."

"Well, excuse me. I still don't see what the problem is. I think it's great that you're in love with Ken."

Jessica sighed dramatically. "Don't you understand anything? Think about it. Right now I want to be with Ken all the time. That's how it always starts. Next thing you know, we'll spend our weekends sitting around in the house in Sweet Valley High sweatshirts, watching sappy old movies on the VCR. Or worse yet, we'll go *bowling*!" She grimaced. "We'll be as boring as you and Todd."

"How would you ever live with yourself?" Elizabeth asked.

"Exactly."

"Jessica, I was joking," Elizabeth explained with a sigh.

"I hate it when you get sarcastic," Jessica complained.

"And I hate it when you criticize me and Todd."

"What's not to criticize?" Jessica shot back.

"This is getting nowhere," Elizabeth said. "Let's talk about something else."

"Fine." Jessica turned the Jeep onto Calico Drive. "Have you decided what you're packing for Catalina?"

"I plan to travel light," Elizabeth said. "Just a few tops, a couple pairs of walking shorts, and maybe a pair of khakis. Oh, and both of my bathing suits."

"Are you crazy? We're staying at a classy resort! We'll go dancing at night, eat at the best restaurants on the island, meet rich, interesting people . . . and you want to do it wearing *walking shorts*?"

"Jessica, the last time I dressed up, it was for John Marin—and look where that got me! I thought *he* was a rich, interesting person." Elizabeth rubbed the sides of her arms. "Just thinking about him now makes my skin crawl. Rich, interesting people are very low on my priority list for this vacation. All I want to do is relax."

Jessica smiled. "While Maria waits tables at the cafe instead of us."

"I'm glad Mr. Jenkins liked her so much at her interview today," Elizabeth said.

"Me, too," Jessica agreed. "Now we won't have to call in every day and pretend we're both sick."

"Jessica! We couldn't have done that!"

"Why not?" Jessica asked breezily. "People do it all the time."

"*I* don't! I'd stay home all week before I did something so dishonest."

"Well, excuse me, Miss Perfect Twin. You didn't seem to mind lying last week when you were sneaking around with Marin," Jessica reminded her sister.

"I wasn't the only one who was sneaking around last week," Elizabeth pointed out. "I seem to remember a certain person who even admitted to breaking into the school through the locker-room window, just to impress a phony television producer."

"Nobody's perfect!" Jessica said cheerfully. Actually, she was secretly glad that Elizabeth had been taken in by Marin, too—and that she also had lied about dating him. Jessica loved her sister more than anything, but at times Elizabeth's good-twin routine got tiring—especially since it implied that Jessica was the evil twin. Of course, Jessica had never wanted to see her sister in danger. She glanced at Elizabeth, and her annoyance dissolved when she remembered how close she'd come to losing her.

"Anyhow," Elizabeth said, "Mr. Jenkins seemed impressed that we took the trouble to find somebody to fill in for us. He said"—she lowered her voice into a reasonable impersonation of their boss—"'It's gratifying to see a person your age who has such a strong sense of responsibility, *Jessica*.' Yes, he called me Jessica. As usual."

27

Jessica laughed as she pulled the Jeep into the driveway of the Wakefield house. "What a jerk! He'll never be able to tell us apart."

"Not unless you dye your hair black again," Elizabeth said, laughing.

"No, thanks," Jessica replied, remembering a time early in the year when she had dyed her hair and changed her image, in order to show everyone that she had an identity apart from her twin. "That was a long, long time ago, when I was young and stupid. Now I know the truth: Blondes really do have more fun. And I plan to prove it this week on Catalina Island."

The twins' mother rifled through the night-gowns in her bureau drawer Friday night, searching for one to take to Santa Catalina. She was looking for something—well, a little romantic. Her husband had been so tense for the past week that he had felt like a stranger. *It's no wonder,* she thought, watching him out of the corner of her eye as he sat on the bed, sorting socks. *He spent the whole week trying to protect his family from a murderer.* She selected a long, elegant gown of aqua silk and folded it gently into her suitcase. *This vacation will do Ned a world of good,* she thought.

Then she shook her head. As concerned as she was about her husband, Mrs. Wakefield had to admit that she was angry with him as well. It was his own fault that he'd spent a week in agony, trying to cope all alone, while his family was in danger. *He should have told me,* she thought.

Suddenly a loud crash echoed through the house, and Mr. Wakefield jumped to his feet. *"What was that noise?"* he shouted, his voice trembling.

Mrs. Wakefield's annoyance abated when she saw the fear in her husband's eyes. "Calm down, Ned," she said in a soothing voice. "I'm sure it's nothing. My guess is that Jessica's trying to pack."

"Ahhh," he murmured, nodding. The chaotic state of Jessica's bedroom was legendary.

"I bet all the shoes and handbags she's got crammed onto the top shelf of her closet just took a flying leap when she pulled out her suitcase."

Mr. Wakefield laughed, but it sounded forced. She crossed the room and stood behind him. "You need to relax, honey," she said, kneading the tense muscles of his shoulders. "You've been on edge for so long."

Her husband groaned appreciatively.

"I still wish you had told me last week that Marin was out of prison and coming after the girls," she said. "We could have helped each other through it."

"Do we have to go over that again, Alice?" he asked. "I told you, I didn't want to scare you."

"Why not? It seems to me that we all had a legitimate reason to be scared. You shouldn't have taken it all on yourself. They're my daughters, too."

"But the whole thing was my responsibility," Mr. Wakefield insisted. "It was only because of me that Marin was stalking the twins."

"You can't blame yourself, Ned. You were just doing your job when you got Marin convicted. You can't honestly tell me that you regret putting him away." Mrs. Wakefield spoke forcefully, but she had repeated the same words so many times that she barely knew what she was saying anymore. Deep inside, she was wondering if an aqua silk nightgown and a week on Catalina Island would be enough to heal the hurt she felt at being excluded from protecting her children.

"No, of course I don't regret sending Marin to prison," her husband replied. "What I regret is that the parole board let him out. I wanted to tell you about it as soon as I read in the newspaper that he was free. But I knew how afraid you'd feel."

"How I would *feel*, Ned?" Mrs. Wakefield asked, her voice rising. "Think about how I felt Sunday morning! I thought I was going to have a heart attack when I pulled into the driveway. Arriving to find four police cars in our driveway, a broken window, and blood on the carpet is not my idea of a pleasant homecoming." She saw his face cloud over and instantly regretted her words. The last thing her husband needed to be reminded of was blood on the carpet. She forced a grin. "And then there was poor Prince Albert, floating around like a helium balloon."

Her husband chuckled, genuinely this time.

The dog had still been feeling the effects of the drugs Marin had given him the night before, to put him to sleep so he wouldn't bark.

She sighed. "I've never been so happy to see you and the girls safe as I was that morning."

"And we were never so happy to be safe. That was some wild night."

"I should have been with you through it," she said, unable to keep the anger from creeping back into her voice. "I'll never understand why you let me go off to Oakland when you knew the girls were in danger."

Mr. Wakefield turned to his wife and put his hands on her shoulders. "I thought you might be in danger, too," he said softly.

Mrs. Wakefield turned away from him and began to fold clothing into her suitcase. "In case you hadn't noticed, Ned," she told her husband, "I'm not a teenager. I have as much right to defend this family as you do. You should have trusted me enough to tell me the truth."

"It's not a question of trust, Alice," Mr. Wakefield said. "We're talking about your safety. Marin said he'd come after the girls *first*. But he threatened you, too."

"Then I have the right to defend myself!" Mrs. Wakefield spoke bravely, but she sat down heavily on the edge of the bed and shuddered. She knew she and her daughters were safe now, but she suddenly felt violently, inexplicably afraid.

31

＊　　＊　　＊

Jessica stood firm beneath the avalanche of shoes and handbags that tumbled down from her closet. She and Elizabeth, standing side by side, had just jerked out her old powder-blue suitcase. Jessica laughed as a black silk scarf drifted downward and draped itself over her sister's face.

Elizabeth swiped the scarf aside. "Honestly, Jessica, I don't know how you can ever find anything in this mess."

"It's easy," Jessica replied. "Everything I own is in plain sight. All I have to do is look around the room, and I can see whatever it is I want." She tossed the suitcase onto her unmade bed. "*I* don't know how *you* can find anything in that echo chamber you call a bedroom."

"I know what you're going to say next," Elizabeth began. She raised her voice to mimic Jessica's more dramatic style of speaking. "*We have nothing at all in common. If we didn't look exactly alike, you'd swear we weren't even rela—*"

"Actually, we have one very big thing in common," Jessica interrupted, suddenly thoughtful. "We both fell for Marin."

"Yes," Elizabeth said in a quiet voice. "We did."

"What was the first thing that attracted you to him?" Jessica asked.

Elizabeth turned toward the window and

shook her head vehemently. "I don't want to think about it."

"But you should," Jessica urged. "You're *supposed* to talk about traumatic things like unhappy love affairs; it helps you analyze what went wrong so you don't fall into the same kind of dysfunctional-relationship pattern again."

Elizabeth spun to stare at her. "Where did you hear that?"

"I read it in *Ingenue* magazine," Jessica answered.

"This is a little more than an unhappy love affair, Jess. This creep tried to murder us! And Dad." She wrapped her arms around herself, as if for warmth."

"Exactly! That's why you have to talk about it." Jessica shoved a huge pile of clothes across the bed to clear a space. Then she flopped down onto the bed, motioning for Elizabeth to take the desk chair.

"Hey!" Elizabeth exclaimed, lifting something blue and wrinkled from the seat. "This is my favorite blouse!"

Jessica shrugged. "Oh, I forgot to tell you—I borrowed your blouse."

"Thanks a lot. I just ironed this!"

Jessica smiled at her sister. "Well, it doesn't look like you did a very good job."

Elizabeth glared at her.

"OK, OK! I'm sorry. I'll iron it for you tonight so you can pack it," Jessica offered.

"No, thanks," Elizabeth said. "Scorch marks aren't in style this season. I'll do it myself."

Jessica grinned. There were advantages to having no domestic skills. She picked through the clothes on the bed until she found the shortest pair of cutoffs she owned and tossed them into the suitcase. "You never answered my question," she persisted. "What was it that attracted you to John Marin?"

Elizabeth took a deep breath. "The first time I saw him, I was with Todd at the Dairi Burger. Todd was getting on my nerves—"

"That's not surprising," Jessica said, arching an eyebrow.

Elizabeth ignored her. "—and I was wondering if Todd and I were really all that compatible. I wished I could find a guy who was my true soul mate." She paused, her eyes glassy.

"And then?"

"And then I looked up, and this amazing-looking guy was sitting by himself in a corner booth, writing in a notebook," Elizabeth continued, staring at her hands. "He had broad shoulders and tousled light-brown hair. He looked up. And our eyes locked, just like in the movies." She turned to her sister, but her voice was so low that Jessica could hardly hear it. "Even from that far away, I could see that his eyes were deep, dark blue."

Jessica shuddered. "They certainly were."

Elizabeth felt a shiver run through her. "Then I had this sudden rock-solid conviction that he was my soul mate—that we were meant to be together."

"If I didn't know you're talking about Marin, I would think that was a terribly romantic story," Jessica said.

"How could he do something like that to me?" Elizabeth asked, tears sprouting in her eyes. "Now just thinking about him makes me want to throw up!"

"Me, too," Jessica said. She rooted through a tangle of panty hose, searching for a pair with no runs. "The first time I saw Marin was at the Marina Cafe," she remembered. "I was mad at you because our shift was over and you were going home."

"Oh, good reason to be mad at me," Elizabeth complained sarcastically.

"I had every right to be mad! You were leaving, but I had to stick around at work, dead on my feet and smelling like french fries. I had this dorky customer who was taking six years to drink one cup of coffee."

Elizabeth rolled her eyes. "And naturally that was my fault."

"OK, maybe that part wasn't your fault," Jessica conceded.

"I wasn't getting along with Todd at all last week, so you probably got the better end of that deal," Elizabeth reminded her.

"Well, you and Todd at least *looked* happy together. I guess I was missing Ken. Then I saw this really hot car pull up outside—a fire-engine-red Mazda Miata."

"Oh, gosh!" Elizabeth exclaimed. "I remember that car! We were pulling out of the parking lot, and Todd went wild over this great sports car that zoomed past us. But we didn't notice the driver."

"That was Marin. Or Scott Maderlake, as he was calling himself." She closed her eyes, remembering the instant attraction she'd felt when he'd walked through the door of the restaurant. Now the thought of him made her skin crawl. "Do you have any panty hose that aren't torn to shreds?" she asked, suddenly desperate to change the subject. "I need to borrow two or three pairs."

"If you planned ahead, you wouldn't be stuck without them at the last minute."

"If I planned ahead, nobody would be able to tell us apart," Jessica replied. "Everybody would call me Elizabeth, like Mr. Jenkins does."

"I give up!" Elizabeth exclaimed. "You can have *one* pair of panty hose—but that's all. I'll get them for you later. But you were telling me about Marin. I suppose you practically threw yourself at him."

"No way!" Jessica objected. "Besides, I didn't have to. He asked me if I could answer some questions about Sweet Valley. It wouldn't have been very friendly of me to refuse, would it?"

"So that's when you started seeing him?"

"We made a date for me to show him around town the next day," Jessica said. "And the rest was history." She held up a strapless red tube dress. "Do you think Dad would have a heart attack if he saw me wear this in public?"

"What is it, a sock with sequins?"

"Very funny," Jessica said with a snort. "It's a dress, dummy. If you had any fashion sense—"

"And if you had any *common* sense—"

Jessica held up her hand. "OK, so I'll take along a jacket to wear over it." She smiled. "Until I'm out of Mom and Dad's sight, that is."

Mrs. Wakefield's golden hair shimmered softly in the darkness. From her slow, regular breathing, her husband knew she was finally asleep. *This past week has been terrible for her*, he thought sadly. *And so much of that is my fault*. At least she was safe now; Marin hadn't touched her. But he sensed a new distance between himself and his wife—a gap he couldn't seem to bridge. *I should have told her about Marin*, he thought. He vowed to make it up to her. It would do them good to spend some time together, with no worries and no responsibilities.

But he couldn't stop horrifying images from flashing through his head: Jessica's eyes widening with fear when she recognized John Marin's photograph as her new boyfriend . . . Elizabeth's scream

37

as she fought for Marin's knife on the deck of the sailing yacht . . . the searing pain that exploded in his temples as Marin bashed him with a board . . . and the glint of Marin's knife as the killer stood over the twins, who had slept together that night in Elizabeth's room.

"I'm never going to fall asleep tonight," he whispered, swinging his legs over the edge of the bed. His wife murmured something and turned on her side. He slipped out of bed and into the hall-way.

The house was utterly silent—as silent as it had seemed at midnight, six days before. That night the peacefulness had been a cruel facade. Deep down, he doubted that he would ever again trust the silence of night.

Elizabeth's door was ajar. Her father stood out-side it, listening to her deep, soft breathing. She was asleep. No doubt Jessica was sleeping, too, be-hind her own door—with Prince Albert stretched across the foot of her rumpled bed. Marin was in prison. Certainly the twins were as safe now as they'd ever been.

Their father's thoughts returned to a time ten years years ago, when he had stood behind the prosecutor's table in the courtroom where Marin had just been sentenced to prison. Hand-cuffs clinked as the police led the murderer away.

"I won't forget you, Wakefield!" Marin shouted

over his shoulder. *"You or your whole family. Your precious little girls will never be safe again!"*

Mr. Wakefield closed his eyes and leaned against the wall outside Elizabeth's room, the plaster cold and smooth against the tense muscles of his back. Following the memory of Marin's threat, a wave of anger, fear, and hatred overwhelmed him—as it had on Saturday night, when he'd stepped through the door and seen the killer leaning over his sleeping daughters. In their sleep the girls had seemed nearly as young as the pretty six-year-olds they'd been when Marin had first threatened them. And just as fragile.

The scene in Elizabeth's bedroom replayed itself in his mind, in slow motion. *Adrenaline rushed through his limbs as he hurled his body into Marin's. And the murderer flew through the window in an explosion of glass.*

"It's over," he had whispered when he'd spotted Marin's crumpled form on the ground below, illuminated by the headlights of police cars.

But now he wondered if it ever really would be.

Chapter 4

"Hey, sugar!" called the brutish inmate in cell 206.

Leighann scowled at him, trying to look taller than she was. Jerry "Pit Bull" Pitts had a face like Frankenstein's and a physique to match. Even behind bars, he could intimidate her. But she was a prison guard. She would not allow the inmates to see that she was afraid.

"Shut up, Pitts!" she demanded in her toughest voice. It was well before dawn on Saturday morning, but Pitts seemed wide-awake and ready for action. Leighann, on the other hand, was only halfway through the night shift, and she was dead tired. She straightened her back and tried to visualize herself as alert and confident—like Clint Eastwood.

"When you gonna come visit me, baby?" Pitts asked. He licked his lips suggestively. "I'd sure make it worth your while."

"Bug off, creep!" Leighann shot back.

"Ooh, listen to her talk tough!" Pitts called, his voice echoing through the cellblock. "It makes me crazy when you do that, honey."

Leighann narrowed her eyes and tried to look menacing. "Go ahead—make my day!" she challenged. "I'll put you on report if you say another word."

"Man, I'm scared now! That would make— what, four times this month?"

"That's it, Pitts. You're going on report!"

"Why don't you come a little closer, baby? I'll give you something to report!"

Leighann felt so frustrated she wanted to scream.

"Leave her alone, Pit Bull!" commanded a deep voice from two cells down. John Marin's voice sounded angry but controlled. "If I hear you giving her a hard time again, I swear I'll make you sorry."

Leighann saw genuine fear in Pit Bull's eyes as he backed away from the bars. "That's right," she told Pit Bull. "You'd better listen to John." She took a deep breath and smoothed the soft wings of frizzy hair that always insisted on breaking free of her guard's hat. Then she walked to Marin's cell.

"Thanks for your help, John," she said softly. "I'll never understand how a guy your size manages to intimidate a goon like Pitts."

"What do you mean, a guy my size?" Marin demanded. He pretended to be insulted, but a grin broke through, making his chiseled features even more handsome. "I'm not exactly a ninety-eight-pound weakling," he reminded her, brushing a lock of light-brown hair from his startlingly dark-blue eyes.

"No, you're certainly not," Leighann said. She glanced over his body admiringly. Marin wasn't nearly as big as Pitts. But he was over six feet tall, and powerfully built. Even the shapeless slate-gray prison uniform couldn't mask his broad shoulders and narrow hips.

Steady, girl, she told herself. *This man may be innocent, but he's still an inmate here.* Leighann was new enough on the job to remember the exact words in the employee manual: *"Fraternizing between inmates and guards is strictly prohibited."*

"So how do you get a guy like Pit Bull to back down?" she asked.

John leaned his head close to the bars, as if he were about to impart a great secret. "Psychology," he said, tapping his temple with his finger. "If you pay attention and learn enough about people, you can figure out what makes them tick and know exactly what to say to have them eating out of your hand."

"I'll have to try it sometime," Leighann said. Suddenly she noticed that Marin had one arm

43

curled protectively around his abdomen. "John, is something the matter? Are you sick?"

John shook his head. "It's nothing. Just some indigestion from last night's dinner. You know—prison food!"

"Don't I know it! We eat the same stuff in the employee cafeteria," Leighann said. "Is that why you're awake so early?"

"Yeah, I guess so," John said. "I've been tossing and turning all night. What was in those sloppy joes? It feels like I've swallowed a handful of rocks."

Leighann peered worriedly into John's cell. "Can I bring you an antacid from the infirmary?" she asked.

"Thanks for being concerned. But don't go to any trouble. I'm sure it'll go away on its own." He smiled so warmly at Leighann that she had to forbid herself to blush. "Seeing you is the best medicine, anyway," he continued. "It doesn't hurt nearly as much as it did before you stopped by."

"Are you sure you don't want me to get you something?"

"I'm sure," he answered. "Besides, I want to talk to you. I made you something in wood shop yesterday."

"That was sweet of you," Leighann said, a little nervously. "But I'm not allowed to accept gifts from inmates."

"I know," he said with a shrug. "But I couldn't

help myself. You've been so kind to me."

She frowned. "Why shouldn't I be? You're the only guy in this whole rotten cellblock who isn't a degenerate."

"And you're the only person in this whole rotten prison who believes in me," he said. "The rest of them think I'm guilty of killing those two men."

"Well, they're wrong," Leighann said staunchly. "My supervisor and the warden keep telling me you're evil. But I know it's not true. You're not a killer, like that worm Pit Bull. Anyone can tell you're innocent just by talking to you."

John shook his head. "Nobody else seems to think so."

"Don't worry," Leighann told him. "It'll all come out at the trial. Once you tell the judge how you were framed, you'll be home free."

John hesitated. "And then," he said, suddenly shy, "I mean, if you want to, the two of us can spend some time together—without bars separating us."

Leighann searched his face for any hint that he might be joking, or just leading her on. She had felt an almost irresistible attraction to John Marin right from the moment she first saw him. But she knew that a lot of good-looking guys were completely insincere; they flirted almost as a matter of habit. *And he's a prison inmate, of all things!* she warned herself. Still, the look in John's eyes was honest, open, and full of affection.

45

"Do you mean that, John?" she asked suspiciously.

"Of course I do," he said, his stunning blue eyes staring directly into hers. "I know it's corny. I've only known you a few days, but being locked up in this place gives a guy a lot of time to think. And all I can think about is you."

Leighann felt a fluttering in her chest, like butterflies. It was the first time John had come close to admitting that he shared the same strong emotions that she felt for him.

From the day they'd met, Leighann had been blown away by John's looks. As she got to know him, she'd decided that his appeal was more than physical—he was a truly nice person, and he always treated her with respect. At first she worried that she was too old for him. After all, Leighann was twenty-three; John didn't look older than twenty. That wasn't an enormous difference, but some guys had a problem with dating older women. Then Leighann had done some checking, and she had learned that he was actually twenty-eight.

Now, with him gazing at her with his mysterious dark-blue eyes, Leighann knew she would fall for him no matter how old he was. "I seem to be thinking about you a lot lately, too," she admitted.

"Does that mean you'll accept the present I made you?" he asked, smiling shyly at her.

Leighann looked down cellblock A to see if

Manuel Ramos, the shift supervisor, was nearby. Manuel wasn't in sight—he was probably doing his rounds of the prisoners on the upper level. "I don't know, John. I've only been in this crummy job two weeks. I can't afford to get in trouble. What if somebody notices me carrying a present from you out of here?"

John smiled. "I already thought of that," he said, pulling a small bundle from beneath his pillow. "This is so tiny, it will fit in your pocket. No one will notice a thing." He stuck it through the bars.

Leighann turned the paper-wrapped package in her hands. "John, you really didn't have to go through the trouble of making me a present. Especially since I don't have anything for you."

"You can owe me one," he said, smiling impishly. "Don't worry—I won't forget to collect."

His gaze made Leighann feel warm all over. Embarrassed, she turned her attention to the bundle in her hands and was surprised to find her fingers trembling as she unwrapped it. She hadn't felt this way about a guy in ages.

"Oh, John!" she breathed. "You *made* this? It's absolutely gorgeous."

In her palm was a perfect, tiny replica of a sailboat. Its miniature sails were so realistic, they seemed to billow in the breeze. "Oh, John," Leighann sighed. "It's lovely."

"To me a sailboat means freedom," John said

quietly. "If I ever get out of this place, I'm going to buy a sailboat and travel anywhere I want to go."

Leighann stared at the beautiful little boat. In her mind it grew to full size. John Marin stood on the deck, his hair tousled from the ocean breeze and his eyes squinting against the sun-gilded waves. "I bet you will, too," she said, unable to keep the wistfulness from creeping into her voice.

"Leighann," John asked, his expression solemn, "if I do get out of here, will you go sailing with me?"

"I would like that," Leighann murmured, deeply moved. She heard a noise at the far end of the cellblock and whirled to see Manuel descending the open spiral staircase from the upper level. "I'll treasure the boat always, John. But I've got to finish my rounds. I'll stop by to see you again before my shift ends, to see how you're feeling."

"Until then I'll think about the two of us together on the ocean, free," he said in a low, sexy tone that left her breathless. "Have you ever been on a moonlight sail, Leighann?"

"I've never even been on a boat," she admitted.

"You'll love it, Leighann," he assured her. "Trust me."

Through the window of her father's rust-brown Ford LTD, Elizabeth watched the safe and sleepy ranch-style houses of Calico Drive glide by in the early-morning sunlight. The neighborhood looked

48

as cheerful and orderly as it always did, but Elizabeth couldn't help feeling that something lurked beneath Sweet Valley's peaceful appearance on that cheerful Saturday morning. Something dangerous.

She shook her head as if to clear the thought from her mind. *Don't be so melodramatic,* she told herself. *Marin is in prison. We don't have to be afraid anymore.*

Her father sighed from the front seat. "It's good to finally be on the road," he said quietly. "It will be a relief to get away from here."

"Oh, my gosh!" Jessica exclaimed suddenly. Her eyes were wide with fear.

Elizabeth saw her father's fingers tense on the steering wheel. "What's the matter?" he asked in a choked voice.

"I forgot to turn on the answering machine!"

Elizabeth laughed. To Jessica, a missed phone call was a major catastrophe. "Oh, no!" she commiserated. "And I thought you were worried about something minor—like a natural disaster."

"This *is* a disaster! What if Ken calls?"

"It's all right, Jess," her mother said, smiling. "*I* turned on the answering machine. But what about Prince Albert? Did you girls find someone to look after him while we're away?"

"It's all taken care of," Elizabeth assured her. "Maria said she and Winston would stop by on their way to the marina every day."

"Winston?" Jessica asked. "Talk about disasters! By the end of the week, Prince Albert will be reeling off one-liners and terrible puns."

"I asked Maria and Winston to take in the mail, too," Elizabeth added. "She has the spare key."

"Thanks, Liz," her mother said. "I completely forgot about the mail. I guess I've been preoccupied."

Elizabeth caught a glimpse of her mother's face in the rearview mirror. Her forehead was wrinkled with tension, as it had been all week.

"*You* shouldn't have had to think about the mail!" Mr. Wakefield snapped. "*I'm* the one who sprang this trip on everyone at the last minute. I should have made all the arrangements. How could I have been so thoughtless?"

Jessica glanced at her twin, and Elizabeth knew that the surprised, worried expression on Jessica's face identically matched her own. Their father was showing the strain of the last week more than anyone. Again Elizabeth noticed the dark circles under his eyes and the tension in his face as he clenched his jaw. "Dad, it's not a big deal," Elizabeth said. "We've taken care of everything."

"*I'm* the one who should be taking care of everything!" Mr. Wakefield exclaimed.

Elizabeth watched her parents from the backseat. Mrs. Wakefield pursed her lips and stared at her husband helplessly, but his gaze was fixed on the road ahead. Elizabeth shifted uncomfortably on the warm vinyl. In front of her, her father was gripping the steering wheel as if he wanted to break it in half.

Suddenly Jessica bounced on the seat like a small child. Her eyes twinkled and a grin lit her face. "I've got it!" she cried. "Let's sing!"

Elizabeth raised an eyebrow. "Sing?"

"You know—traveling songs!"

"But nobody in this family can carry a tune," Elizabeth objected. "Especially you."

"Good!" Jessica said. "Since we're all tone-deaf, we won't be able to tell how off-key we are."

"Jessica, I don't think—" her mother began.

"Come on, everybody—sing along!" Jessica interrupted. She raised her hands and began waving them as if she were conducting an invisible band. *"Cat-a-lin-a, here I come, right back where I started from. . . ."*

Elizabeth smiled and then began to giggle. Nobody could resist Jessica's good humor for long. She opened her mouth and joined in, singing as enthusiastically and as tunelessly as her sister.

Leighann yawned as she checked her watch. "Eight o'clock in the morning," she mumbled sleepily to herself. *Less than an hour until I can go home and finally get some shut-eye.* She simply had to find a way to get transferred to the day shift.

Well, there is one advantage to working nights,

51

she thought, casting a cold glare at an inmate who whistled as she walked by. *At least this place is as quiet as a tomb for most of my shift. Too bad the prisoners wake up before I leave.*

She smiled as she caught sight of another advantage to her job. John Marin was sitting on his bed in cell 202. She turned to see if her supervisor was nearby; she didn't want Manuel to know how close she was getting to the handsome young prisoner. She was in luck. The supervisor was nowhere to be seen.

"Hi, John!" she said cheerfully. "How're you feeling? Any better?"

John didn't answer. He was leaning over awkwardly, as if trying to tie his shoelaces.

"John?" Leighann asked. "Are you all right? *John?*"

With agonizing slowness, John turned his head to look at her. His face was twisted in pain. "Just . . . indigestion," he whispered, clutching his stomach. "I'll be OK in a minute."

"It doesn't look like indigestion to me," Leighann protested. "And you're *not* OK!" She pulled the cellular intercom from her belt. "I'd better buzz the infirmary and have them send a doctor up right away."

"No!" John croaked. "I'm fine . . . really." Then his body rolled to one side, and John Marin collapsed onto the floor.

* * *

"Oh, give me a home where the buffalo roam," Jessica sang as the Wakefields' car cruised down the freeway, "where the water-skiers and the Windsurfers play. Where seldom is heard a discouraging word, and the guys flex their muscles all day!"

"Very inspiring," Elizabeth said in what Jessica thought of as her superior-twin voice. "I'm glad you appreciate the natural wonders of the channel islands."

Jessica sighed. "You don't have to sound so sarcastic. You say that you only have eyes for Todd. But I've seen you scoping out the guys on the beach at home."

Mrs. Wakefield grinned from the front seat, and Jessica noticed that the tension was finally smoothing away from her mother's face. "You can't expect your sister to sit on the beach with her eyes closed," Mrs. Wakefield pointed out.

"Exactly," Jessica said. "She just doesn't like to admit it."

"OK, OK. So I sneak a peek now and then," Elizabeth said. "Sue me."

Mrs. Wakefield glanced mischievously at her husband. "Personally, I plan to keep my eyes wide-open on Catalina this week."

"Oooh, Dad!" Jessica called. "I hope you brought your new swim trunks!"

"What was that?" the twins' father asked, still sounding distracted. At least, Jessica thought, he was no longer clenching the steering wheel as if it were Marin's neck.

"Never mind," Mrs. Wakefield said, watching him. "Here's San Pedro. This is where we catch the boat."

"How long is the boat trip?" Elizabeth asked, her voice suddenly lowered almost to a whisper.

"Only about an hour," Mrs. Wakefield replied. Jessica saw her mother's worried eyes watching Elizabeth in the rearview mirror.

Elizabeth sank back in the seat and turned to stare out the window. Jessica looked at her curiously. For the first time in a week, the twins and their mother had seemed relaxed. Mr. Wakefield still looked tense, but even he was beginning to loosen up. Now, all of a sudden, Elizabeth looked scared again. Jessica followed her sister's stare and finally understood. Elizabeth's eyes were fixed on the sleek white lines of the channel boat as the Wakefields drove closer to the dock. She was afraid of the boat. In Elizabeth's mind, Jessica realized, she was back on the deck of that other boat, fighting for her life.

This won't do, Jessica thought. She had to find a way to cheer up her sister and get her mind off the evening on Marin's yacht. Jessica pointed to the harbor. "There's the channel boat! Awesome! Can we sit on the front part, near the railing?" she asked in a bubbly voice. "I want the guys on the beach at Catalina to see me coming."

Elizabeth laughed. "Honestly, Jessica, you've got such a one-track mind!"

"Oh, well," Jessica said with a smile. "At least my one track has got some great scenery along it!"

Leighann frantically fumbled with her keys. She knew there was a correct procedure for dealing with inmates who needed medical attention, but she had no time to worry about procedures. This was a life-or-death situation.

"John?" she called as she tried the wrong key in the lock. "Talk to me, John!"

The prisoner's body lay still on the floor of the cell. Leighann couldn't tell if he was breathing.

Finally the lock clicked. Leighann shoved the door open and knelt beside the prostrate form. "Oh, John! Please don't be dead, John! Please don't be dead!"

She heard a few voices from the cells around her—some concerned, others mocking—but she had no time for the other prisoners. She suddenly realized that she was completely in love with John Marin. And now he might be dead, or dying. She leaned close, holding her hand near his mouth to check for breathing, while she took Marin's wrist in her other hand to see if he had a pulse.

Suddenly his wrist sprang to life and flicked around to grab her hand.

"Thank heaven!" she began with a sigh. "I thought—"

"Shut up," he hissed into her ear. She felt him whisk her gun out of its shoulder holster.

"John, what is this? If this is some kind of a joke—"

"It's no joke, darling," he whispered, expertly tying her hands together to the bedpost with a rope that Leighann guessed he'd made from his sheet. He yanked the cell phone from her belt. "Call that supervisor of yours," he ordered. "Tell him to come here now, alone."

"John! I don't understand."

He shoved the gun painfully into her chest. "If you try anything funny, I'll kill you."

Leighann nodded, her eyes wide. She could barely catch her breath. Through her uniform shirt, the barrel of the gun was cold and hard against her chest—almost as cold and hard as John's eyes.

"Uh, Manuel," she said into the receiver, wondering if the supervisor could hear her heart pounding through the receiver. "I need you down here for a moment. Can you meet me at number two-oh-two?"

"What's the problem this time, LeShay?" Manuel asked, an edge of annoyance in his voice.

"I'm, um, not quite sure," Leighann stammered. "I think Marin's sick, but I can't tell if it's serious enough to call the infirmary."

"I'm a prison guard, not a doctor," he said. "Let the professionals decide."

The gun barrel pressed harder against her breastbone, and Leighann gasped. "Please, Manuel! I'd feel a lot better if you'd come take a look." She was so surprised that John was treating her roughly that she barely knew what she was saying on the phone. The man she thought she loved was actually *hurting* her.

"I get it," Manuel said. "Another crisis like last week, when the guy in cell three-oh-nine had athlete's foot."

Leighann desperately tried to focus and think up an argument that might convince her boss to come to Marin's cell. "If you call the doctor and there's nothing really wrong with Marin," she pointed out, "then we're both going to look pretty silly, aren't we?" She felt close to tears with pain and disappointment, but she knew her voice sounded relatively normal.

Manuel sighed. "All right, Leighann. I'm on my way."

Mr. Wakefield breathed deeply and gazed over the ship's prow. The salt-tinged air felt fresh in his lungs, and the warm breeze that swept over his face was pure and cleansing. For the first time in two weeks, he felt free.

His wife held on to his arm and snuggled against him, strands of her golden hair blowing across his neck and chest. She smiled up at him. "This was a great idea," she said. "We're not even on the island yet, and already I feel a hundred percent better."

"Me, too," he replied. "For the first time all week, I don't feel as if I should be looking over my shoulder—not to mention keeping an eye on the girls twenty-four hours a day."

Jessica and Elizabeth were standing a few yards to his left. Over the buffeting of the wind, their father could hear only occasional snatches of the twins' conversation. It sounded as if Jessica was entertaining her sister with a lively patter about the shopping, the sights, and the boys of Catalina. Elizabeth was giggling so hard she had to lean on the ship's railing for support.

Then Mr. Wakefield noticed the way that Jessica was protectively holding on to her sister's arm, much the same way that his wife held his own. Suddenly he realized what Jessica was doing. Elizabeth hadn't said anything to her parents, but her father knew she'd been afraid of being on a boat again. Now her fear seemed forgotten as she laughed at her sister's silly commentary.

As usual, his wife knew exactly what he was thinking. "I see that Jessica is determined to keep Elizabeth's mind off last weekend," Mrs. Wakefield murmured into his ear. "And it seems to be working. I haven't seen Elizabeth laugh like that all week."

"She's lucky to have somebody nearby who cares that much about her," the twins' father said, looking into his wife's beautiful blue eyes. "I know from personal experience how much of a difference that can make."

"How are you feeling?"

He brushed a strand of hair from his wife's eyes. Then he leaned down and kissed her gently on the lips. "Much, much better," he said. "You know, I really believe we're going to be able to put this all behind us."

Marin lay tense on his cot, peering out from under the thin prison-issue blanket. Outside the cell, he could hear approaching footsteps echoing down the corridor.

"Remember, darling," he whispered to Leighann, "I've got your piece right here in my hand." From below, he poked the barrel of the nine-millimeter handgun against the blanket. "If you say anything wrong when your friend Manuel gets here, I'll blow away your pretty little head."

Through a wrinkle in the blanket, he caught a glimpse of Leighann's wide-eyed nod. He felt a rush of gratitude toward the young prison guard, mixed with contempt. She had certainly made his work easier by falling in love with him. And her looks didn't hurt, either. He studied her from his woolen cavern. Leighann's eyes were large and dark, and her clear skin was the color of hot chocolate. Her black hair was frizzy and untamed, making her features appear even sweeter and more innocent in contrast.

Now she crouched by the side of the cot, as if leaning over Marin to check on his condition. Marin had draped the blanket so that one corner fell over her wrists; from the cell's entrance, Manuel wouldn't be able to see that her hands were tied. Of course, her gun was missing from her shoulder holster. But with luck Manuel wouldn't notice that until it was too late.

The footsteps came closer and then stopped. Marin sensed that the supervisor was standing directly outside the cell.

"Dammit, LeShay," came Manuel's deep, weary voice. "You know the rules. What are you doing in a prisoner's cell? And with the door unlocked!"

"Forget the rules!" Leighann answered, her voice quavering. "This is a life-or-death matter."

Marin held his breath, out of anxiety as much as anything. Would Manuel take the bait?

Manuel's voice seemed uncertain. "I swear, LeShay, you exaggerate more than anyone I've ever met. It's probably nothing. I'll call the infirmary."

"No!" Leighann cried. "There's no time! I can't tell if he's breathing!"

"OK, let me see what we've got."

Manuel leaned over the bed and pulled the blanket from Marin's face. As he did, Marin leaped from the cot and caught him in a stranglehold.

"Drop your gun and your intercom on the cot," Marin ordered. He jabbed Manuel's spine with Leighann's weapon. "Now!"

The supervisor began to shudder in the stranglehold. Manuel's eyes grew round and filled with a sick sense of realization as he stared into Marin's face.

"And if you make a sound," Marin continued, "you and the little lady here are both dead."

Manuel's fingers were trembling as he pulled the intercom from his belt and tossed it onto the bed. Marin nodded toward the gun. The only sound in the cell was metal sliding against leather as Manuel slipped the weapon from its holster. His eyes were riveted to Marin's face, as if hoping to catch the inmate in a moment's distraction. Marin sneered, and Manuel lowered his gaze. With a last, wistful glance at his weapon, Manuel dropped it onto the cot.

Then Marin swung an arm around to bash Manuel in the side of the head with Leighann's gun. Leighann stifled a scream as her boss dropped to the floor, scarlet streaming down the side of his face.

Marin knelt beside Manuel and felt his pulse. Then he began unbuttoning the man's guard uniform.

"Is he dead?" Leighann whimpered.

"He's dead," Marin said flatly, yanking Manuel's arms from his uniform jacket.

"What are you doing to him?" Leighann choked out.

"Shut your mouth," Marin barked. "Unless you want to end up like your boss."

Marin quickly pulled on Manuel's uniform jacket. His own prison pants were a close enough color to pass for a guard's pants. Then he untied Leighann's bonds. "Get up and do exactly as I say," he ordered, smiling coldly. "Darling, it's time for our moonlight sail."

Chapter 5

The door to her office opened, and Marianna West looked up from the conference table. Her mouth puckered in distaste when she saw who was entering. "Hello, Griffin," she said in a controlled voice. She pointed to the clock on the wall. "I was expecting you nearly two hours ago. It's almost eleven."

Griffin Pierce wiped his high, shiny forehead. He was only thirty years old, but his receding hairline made him look closer to fifty. "Lighten up, Marianna. It's Saturday morning! And I don't appreciate having this case dumped on me at the last minute, just so Ned could go on vacation."

"You don't have to appreciate it," she said sweetly. "You're an associate, Griffin. Ned's a partner. And so, I might mention, am *I*," she added pointedly. "Besides, you know what Ned's been through in the last week. His family needs to get away." At that moment Marianna wished she, too, could get away—from Griffin.

"So what do you need me to work on?" he asked with a resigned sigh.

She held out a folder. "I need six copies of these records," she said. At least if Griffin was photocopying papers, he would be out of her office.

"*Copies?*" Griffin asked, in shock. "You want *me* to photocopy files? Man, am I glad I went to law school to prepare for this."

Marianna glared at him, and Griffin's mouth snapped shut. He snatched the papers from her and stalked out of the room. Marianna sighed happily after he had gone. Without Griffin in it, the office seemed extraordinarily peaceful.

"Oh, we'll all have chicken and dumplings when she comes!" Harry Emerson sang as he drove the family car through the desert late Saturday morning. It wasn't quite lunchtime, but he was feeling awfully hungry. Chicken and dumplings would pretty much hit the spot.

Unfortunately, he realized, he and his family were in California now—the land of bean sprouts and pita bread. There probably wasn't a single dumpling between there and home, American Fork, Utah.

"Daddy! You stopped singing in the middle!" complained five-year-old Margie from the flat, decklike part of the station wagon, the section the kids called "the way back."

"Lucky for us," said Harry, Jr., staring glumly out the window. At eleven years old, Harry, Jr., was just too cool for family vacations—and easily embarrassed by fathers who sang in public. Even if the public, in this case, was only his family.

Harry, Sr., patted his potbelly. "How about stopping for lunch soon?" he asked. "I'm getting pretty darn hungry."

"Dear, it's only eleven o'clock," replied his wife, Beatrice. "I thought we were going to wait until Los Angeles to eat lunch. If we stop now, we'll upset our whole schedule."

Harry sighed. Beatrice didn't like doing anything unexpected. Usually Harry went along with her. But today he was feeling rebellious. "Is that such a terrible thing?" he asked hesitantly. "I mean, does it really matter if we eat at eleven instead of twelve thirty?"

"Of course it matters! Margie is only five. Children's systems are very sensitive to changes in routine."

"Yes, I guess you're right," he said meekly. "What was I thinking?"

From the corner of his eyes, Harry watched his wife, who was sitting smugly on the seat beside him. As always, Beatrice had been confident that he would do exactly as she wanted. He gripped the steering wheel tighter. He was tired of living by her rules. Right then and there, he made a decision. Sometime on this vacation, he vowed, he would do something completely unexpected—something that would drive Bea crazy.

Leighann lay on the floor of her Geo Metro, wincing as Marin tied her wrists together.

"Hey!" she yelled. "You're cutting off my circulation!"

"Sorry, darling," Marin said with a smile, loosening the bonds a little. "I didn't mean to hurt you." Leighann noticed that he had reverted back to his polite, gentlemanlike self, now that they were away from the prison and he was free. *If the words "polite" and "gentlemanlike" can be used to describe a guy who would make you fall in love with him, and then murder your boss, kidnap you, and force you to drive him into the desert,* she thought grimly.

"What's going to happen now?" Leighann asked.

"Well," John began, "now that the car is hidden in this canyon, far off the road, I plan to leave you here in it—and then to be on my way. So don't trouble your mind about me anymore, darling."

"I'm not your darling!" Leighann yelled. She could hardly believe what was happening to her. Just twelve hours earlier she'd been dreaming of having a real relationship with this creep. Now she wished she'd never met him. She still couldn't believe she'd been so blind to his true character.

"Don't be mad, baby," Marin said in a soothing voice. He reached down to stroke her face.

Leighann caught sight of her own gun sticking out of his belt. Once again her mind replayed the image of the blood on Manuel's face as he lay on the floor of cell 202, his skin as pale as bone. She shuddered and twisted her face away from Marin's touch. The warden and poor Manuel had been right. Marin was evil. And she had been taken in by him. She had even believed he could fall in love with her. *How could I have been such an idiot?* she chided herself. "Don't you dare touch me!" she ordered bravely, fighting back her tears.

"I'm sorry, Leighann," Marin said simply. "You don't have to be afraid of me. I won't hurt you." The desert sun, almost directly overhead, plucked golden highlights from his hair as he stood in the car doorway, but his face was in shadow.

"Why should I believe you, after what you did to Manuel?" she demanded.

He began tying her ankles. "I needed Manuel dead. He would have sounded the alarm."

"I wish I had," she said, glowering at him.

Marin went on as if she hadn't spoken. "I needed you to get me through the prison security system. Also, I knew you had a car—transportation away from that rat hole. Of course, I can't risk going any farther in your car now. They'll be searching all the roads for it. So I'll have to locate some alternate transportation."

"So you don't need me anymore. Does that mean you're going to kill me?" Leighann was surprised at how flat and matter-of-fact her voice sounded.

Marin shrugged. "Killing you would serve no purpose. You don't know where I'm heading, so you can't talk. By the time anyone finds you in this desert, my trail will be cold."

"I get it," Leighann said bitterly. "You don't pull the trigger, so you think my death won't be on your conscience. But I'll still die out here in the middle of nowhere. You know it as well as I do."

Marin shook his head. "No, you won't, sweetheart. We're only a few miles from the prison. Somebody will find you."

"Right. After it's too late."

"I'll give you a hint," Marin said. "Keep working at the ropes. You'll be able to loosen them by tonight—probably enough to get your hands free."

Leighann grimaced. "This is the desert! It'll be a hundred thirty degrees in this car by afternoon. If it takes me too long to die of thirst, I'll fry to death first."

"No, you won't, sugar," Marin told her with an amused grin. "This canyon's in shade almost all day long. Trust me, darling. I wouldn't let anything bad happen to you."

"Right," Leighann fumed. "You're a real

humanitarian. I trusted you before—and look where it got me!"

"Once you're free, forget about driving straight to the authorities," Marin continued. "I've slashed all your tires. And by the time you walk to the main road, I'll be far away from here."

Suddenly Leighann's anger fell away like a mask. She felt more depressed than she'd ever been in her life. Everything was clear now. From the moment they'd met, every word out of Marin's mouth had been an act. He'd planned his whole escape around her. He'd manipulated her into falling in love with him, to make her want to rush into his cell when she thought he was dying. He'd used her—not only to escape, but also to kill Manuel. And she'd helped him all the way.

"I thought you liked me," she said as tears began streaming down her face.

"I do like you. And I'm grateful for your help in busting out of that place. That's why I'm going to give you a little career advice: Don't get too close to the prisoners." He winked. "They're scum."

"My career as a prison guard is over!" Leighann screamed. "I'm quitting my job the second I get back to that rat hole—right before the warden opens his mouth to fire me."

"I'm really sorry about this next part," Marin said, leaning toward her. He held a satin scarf that he must have found in the trunk of her car. The long scarf was stretched out in Marin's hands, and

Leighann's eyes widened as she realized the truth. He was going to strangle her with it. Marin had lied about letting her live, just as he had lied about everything else. Leighann's entire body went numb with horror.

Her scream was sliced short as Marin stuffed the scarf into her mouth.

"I hate to have to gag you," he said. "But it's a necessary precaution. I can't have you screaming for help, can I?"

"Mmmpphh!"

Marin smiled as if he were dropping her off for tea at the Ritz-Carlton Hotel. "I have to say good-bye, sweetheart. You'll be a lot more comfortable if you don't panic too much." He blew her a kiss. *"Arrivederci!"*

The car door slammed shut, and Marin sauntered away, the sound of his jaunty whistling fading into the hot, dry breeze. Leighann was alone. In fact, in her whole life she had never felt so lonely. Or so betrayed.

Tears started rolling down her cheeks, and that made her angry again. She was angry at Marin for betraying her, but she was even more angry at herself. She couldn't believe she'd been so stupid and so trusting—and that she had liked him enough to feel so hurt, even now.

In defiance of Marin's last suggestion, Leighann shifted awkwardly in the cramped space. Something small and hard in her pocket jabbed into her hip.

She tried to change her position, but she couldn't seem to move away from the object.

Then she remembered what was in her pocket—a perfect miniature replica of a sailboat, carved in wood. To Marin it had meant freedom. To Leighann it brought only pain.

"Awesome!" Jessica cried, surveying the central courtyard of the Hotel Orizaba as the Wakefields searched for their rooms.

Sparkling adobe walls stretched around three sides of the piazza, rising two and three stories above the ground. Within those walls, pillared colonnades held private balconies that overlooked a swimming pool. Above it all, a peaked roofline of red tile shone in the midday sun.

"It's wonderful, Ned," the twins' mother murmured, leaning close to her husband.

Even Mr. Wakefield's nervous tension had finally lifted. "Yes, it is," he agreed, giving her a peck on the cheek. "And we're going to have a wonderful time here."

Jessica caught sight of a tall, bronzed body in swim trunks diving into the pool. "I think I'm going to have a great time here, too," she said with a smile.

On the far end of the pool, four teenagers played badminton. At tables scattered throughout the courtyard, relaxed-looking people with great tans sipped colorful drinks, as if posing for a cranberry-juice-cocktail commercial.

Jessica bounced on her toes. "What do we do first?"

Elizabeth cocked her head. "Unpack?"

Jessica's mouth dropped open. "Of all the boring—" she began. Then she saw that her sister was laughing.

"It's eleven thirty," Elizabeth said, checking her watch. "How about a swim in the pool first, and then a late lunch?"

"Now you're talking!" Jessica said. "And there's our room, right here on the first floor—number one-fourteen. Come on! I'll race you into our bathing suits!"

"Girls, we're next door in room one-twelve," the twins' father said, sliding the electronic key into the slot beside the door. "Knock when you're ready, and I'll come down to the pool with you."

Jessica sighed. The anxious look on her father's face did not bode well for her social life. He was likely to spend the whole week hovering over her and Elizabeth, scaring away all the great-looking guys.

Her mother obviously had a similar thought. She gently placed a hand on her husband's shoulder. "Ned, the girls don't need a bodyguard," she said softly. "Marin is locked up, and we can all finally relax."

Harry Emerson scratched his head and stared down the empty desert road. The last few puffs of dust vanished in the distance, beneath heat waves that rippled in the air like snakes.

"That was awesome!" Harry, Jr., declared. "That hitchhiker had a real gun! How totally cool!"

Harry, Sr., shook his head. "Son, this isn't the time—"

"Daddy!" Margie cried, tugging on his pant leg. One thumb was in her mouth. "Why did that man take our car?"

"You had to be the big risk taker!" Beatrice yelled, pointing a finger at Harry. "You had to do an idiotic thing like pick up a hitchhiker. You said it would be an adventure. Well, it's an adventure all right! It could be hours before another car comes along."

"Wow, this is so cool!" Harry, Jr., exclaimed. "Does that mean we get to walk through the desert, all the way to Los Angeles? Wait until the kids at school hear about this!"

Harry gazed at the horizon, half expecting the clean-cut young hitchhiker to make a U-turn in their wood-paneled station wagon and race back to the Emersons. The hitchhiker's eyes would crinkle with laughter as he explained that he'd only been joking.

But the horizon was clear. The hitchhiker was gone, along with the Emersons' car, their cash, and much of their luggage. Harry sighed, trying to tune out his wife's litany of charges. *Risk taking*, he decided, *isn't all it's cracked up to be*. On their next vacation, he'd carry traveler's checks.

Griffin was driving Marianna crazy.

"This case shouldn't be going to court at all," he argued, sitting with her in her office at the law firm early Saturday afternoon. "The client ought to settle."

Marianna heard her own voice rising. "He doesn't want to settle! He's more interested in justice than in money."

"Great," Griffin said sarcastically. "And our percentage of his justice comes to how much?"

"Excuse me?" questioned a new voice from the doorway. A clean-cut young man with light-brown hair stood at the threshold, carrying a metal toolbox. "Is this Ned Wakefield's office?"

"Right firm, wrong office," Marianna said, grateful for the distraction. "Ned's on vacation. Can I help you?"

"I'm sorry to bother you on a Saturday," the man said with an apologetic grin. "But I'm with your voice-mail company." He consulted a notebook. "I got a call late yesterday from a Trudy Roman, your office manager. She said Mr. Wakefield was having trouble with his voice mail."

"I didn't know the voice-mail people worked on weekends," Marianna said.

"It must be in your service contract," the man said. "Has anyone else experienced voice-mail problems?"

"Not that I know of," Marianna said. "Well, Mr.

Pierce will show you to Mr. Wakefield's telephone," she offered. She raised her eyebrows at the associate. "Griffin, remember the policy on weekend visitors in the offices."

Unauthorized personnel weren't allowed in the office during off-hours, unless accompanied by an employee. Griffin would have to wait in Wakefield's office—no doubt bored out of his mind—while the phone man fixed the voice mail. Marianna felt a perverse sense of satisfaction from the look of annoyance in Griffin's eyes.

John Marin pretended to be placing a test call from Mr. Wakefield's office. In reality he was watching out of the corner of his eye the obnoxiously preppy attorney who had escorted him there and who now leaned against the doorjamb. Griffin Pierce, the tall, attractive woman had called him. Even his name sounded stuffy.

"This may take a few minutes," Marin said, disguising his contempt with a cheerful voice.

"Oh, there's no rush," Griffin responded with a sneer. "I'm only an associate. I've got nothing better to do. Not like those busy, important partners."

Marin sized the man up instantly. He cocked his head in the direction of the woman's office. "She sure gets up a full head of steam," he remarked conspiratorially.

"That's an understatement," Griffin replied. "I sweat through years of law school, and the Ice

Queen expects me to do her photocopying!"

"Women bosses are the pits!" Marin sympathized. "Hey, I know how boring this must be for you, standing around watching me push buttons. If you want to sneak out for a cup of coffee or something—"

Griffin slumped against the door frame. "I can't," he said glumly. "Company policy."

Marin grinned. "I won't say anything to you-know-who."

Griffin peeked down the hallway through the open door, then gave Marin a thumbs-up signal. "I'll be back in ten minutes," he said.

As soon as Griffin had gone, closing the door behind him, Marin tapped into voice mail. There wasn't a thing wrong with Mr. Wakefield's telephone. Yet.

"Please enter your security code," ordered a mechanical-sounding female voice over the phone line.

"Dammit!" Marin whispered, staring at the closed door. "What would Wakefield use as his security code?" He thought back to conversations he'd had with white-collar criminals in the state prison. Most people used four to ten characters for passwords, spelling out something they knew they'd remember. He punched in the letters A-L-I-C-E.

"That is not a valid security code," chastised the recorded voice on the line.

"Come on, Ned," Marin said aloud to a framed family photograph on Wakefield's desk. "What's your security code? I know—you live on Calico Drive. How about C-A-L-I-C-O?" He jabbed at the letters.

That is not a valid security code.

"Talk to me, Ned!" he ordered the photograph. Then he batted it aside. "If I were Ned Wakefield, what word would I choose? He tried S-T-E-V-E-N, the names of both girls, and then, thinking of the Wakefield family dog, even A-L-B-E-R-T. No luck. And he didn't have much time. That windbag Griffin Pierce would be back soon.

Suddenly Marin smiled at the receiver. "I've got you now, Wakefield!" His fingers skipped over the keys as he typed in T-W-I-N-S.

Your voice mail is on, the computerized voice said. *You have one message. Dial five to listen to your message.*

"Yes!" Marin cried in a stage whisper.

The message was from Detective Cabrini, the police officer who had arrested him at the Wakefield house the night he'd crashed through Elizabeth's window.

"Ned, I know you're vacationing on Santa Catalina, but I don't know which hotel," Cabrini said in a frantic voice. "I hope you'll phone in to the office for your messages. I've got urgent news, and it's not good."

Marin smiled. *Not good? That all depends on*

77

your perspective, Detective, he thought.

"Marin is out!" Cabrini continued. "He escaped from prison this morning. The warden still doesn't know how that lunatic managed it, but he left one guard dead—bashed the man's head in."

"No big loss," Marin said, narrowing his eyes to slits. Manuel had been one of those domineering, by-the-book guards that Marin hated.

"He kidnapped another guard," Cabrini said. "She's a twenty-three-year-old woman who had only been on the job for two weeks. As far as we know, Marin left with her, in her car. He's probably headed into the desert. The warden called in an all-points bulletin. And the police and the FBI are scouring the place now, for some sign of Marin or the car—" He paused. "Or the guard's body."

Marin grinned. "Now, would I do a rotten thing like that to a harmless little twit like LeShay?" he asked, as if he expected an answer from the detective's recorded voice.

"Call me as soon as you receive this message," Cabrini ended. "If Marin's smart, he's already hundreds of miles away from here. But he still might come after your daughters again. Call me from Catalina, and we'll work out a plan to keep them safe."

"Catalina Island?" Marin said thoughtfully.

He keyed a code into the voice-mail system to erase Cabrini's message. Then he punched in another code to have any future calls forwarded to a phony number. The next time Cabrini called, his message would be sent harmlessly into cyberspace. The Wakefields would continue to believe that Marin was tucked away safely in his prison cell. *Until it's too late,* he thought, chuckling to himself.

Marin rifled through the papers on Mr. Wakefield's desk until he found one with the name of a hotel on Catalina Island.

"The Hotel Orizaba," he murmured. "Not bad! I've got to hand it to you, Counselor, you sure know how to show the ladies a good time. You know, a week in prison has absolutely ruined my tan. Maybe an island vacation is just what I need."

Chapter 6

Mr. Wakefield smiled and stretched out on a chaise lounge next to his wife's. He shaded his eyes from the bright afternoon sun as he turned to look at her. For the first time in a week, she seemed truly relaxed and happy. The dark circles were fading from beneath her eyes, and her forehead had lost the pinched look it had worn since the morning she'd returned from Oakland to find her household in an uproar.

"Hi!" said a perky voice. A shadow fell across Mr. Wakefield's legs, and a bouncy college-age woman with straight black hair and almond-shaped eyes smiled down at him. "I'm Debbie Clayton, and I'm your poolside hostess this afternoon! Can I get either of you anything to drink? Seltzer? Iced tea? A wine spritzer?"

"Iced tea would be lovely," Mrs. Wakefield said.

The twinkle in her eyes told her husband that she found the girl's enthusiasm as amusing as he did.

"I'll have the same," Mr. Wakefield said.

Debbie bounced away, and the Wakefields cracked up.

"Were we ever that young?" Mrs. Wakefield asked after they'd caught their breath.

"I never was," her husband said, turning on his side to get a better view of his wife. "But you look as if you still could be." He could have sworn that his wife had hardly aged at all in twenty years of marriage. Her golden hair, so much like her daughters', was untouched by gray. Her eyes were as blue as the cool water of the hotel swimming pool. And her figure, in her modest but flattering aqua swimsuit, was still slender.

She pointed to the pool. "The twins sure seem to be settling into things here."

Her husband followed her gaze. Jessica was wading into the shallow end of the pool, wearing a blue-and-white bikini so skimpy he would have outlawed it if he'd seen it earlier. She nonchalantly wandered into a raucous game that seemed to have no rules or boundaries, except that it involved a beach ball and two handsome teenage boys. Mr. Wakefield shook his head. Even after a week of dating a murderer, Jessica had the guts—or was it recklessness?—to seek out strange guys.

Elizabeth, as industrious as always, executed a perfect dive from the low board and began swimming laps on the other end of the pool. Her racing-style swimsuit, in green-and-blue plaid, was stylish but practical.

Suddenly the twins' father jumped to his feet. A young man with light-brown hair was wading quickly toward Elizabeth, churning up ripples in his wake. His height and muscular build seemed familiar—*like John Marin's*.

"Elizabeth!" her father yelled, knocking over a plastic table as he leaped toward the pool.

Elizabeth and Jessica both stopped in the water and turned toward him, mortified. Meanwhile, the man with light-brown hair jumped out of the water to catch a Frisbee that was spinning above Elizabeth's head.

Elizabeth looked from Mr. Wakefield to the Frisbee player and shook her head slightly at her father. Jessica was more blatant. She threw her father a dirty look as the two handsome boys with the beach ball eyed him warily.

"Oh, Ned," came his wife's sad voice from behind him.

Mr. Wakefield slumped back to his chair. "I thought I was finally relaxed," he began. "I thought I was over last week. But when I saw that guy running toward Elizabeth, I thought—"

"I know what you thought," Mrs. Wakefield said. "But I will not put up with this kind of behavior all week, Ned. I'm putting my foot down. No watching the twins like a hawk!"

"I know they deserve to have some fun after last weekend," he conceded. "But I've got this feeling—"

"The girls are perfectly safe!" Alice objected.

Mr. Wakefield sighed. "I know, I know. And you're absolutely right. I need to chill out, as Jess would say. I have to let them enjoy their freedom. But it's not going to be easy."

John Marin sat in the stern of the channel boat, watching San Pedro recede over the water as the boat headed to Catalina Island. The salt smell of the ocean and the cries of gulls reminded him of the rented sailing yacht he'd docked at Sweet Valley Marina.

His moonlight sail with Elizabeth had been only one week earlier, but it seemed like a long, long time ago. Something about being in prison made time stretch out endlessly, so that a week might as well be a year. At twenty-eight, Marin knew he had a lot of time ahead of him, but he seethed about every day he'd wasted sitting in a nine-by-nine cell. It was all Ned Wakefield's fault—all those wasted days and wasted nights.

A few weeks earlier, after ten long years of prison, Marin had finally been paroled. He should have had enough time to accomplish his goal, but he had failed. Elizabeth and Jessica Wakefield were alive and well. Their father still had his happiness and peace of mind. *Not for long*, Marin promised himself. Soon that peace of mind would be shattered. The Wakefields' happy life would be nothing more than a gut-wrenching memory.

The day was warm, but the sea breeze was cool as it buffeted the open deck. Marin untied Harry Emerson's new Death Valley sweatshirt from around his waist and pulled it on over the blue-and-white-plaid shirt he was wearing. He'd found both in the suitcase Emerson had left in that god-awful wood-paneled station wagon. Plaid wasn't Marin's style, but it was a lot less conspicuous than a prison guard's uniform.

He decided he would buy some clothes on the island. He'd pick up a pair of jeans, at least, as soon as he arrived. His gray prison-issue pants were nondescript. But now that he was out, he'd prefer to savor his freedom in civilian clothes. For all their shortcomings, the Emersons at least had traveled with plenty of cash—enough cash to keep Marin in style on Catalina Island for a few days.

"And a few days is all I'll need," he vowed, "to make sure this is the last vacation the Wakefield twins ever take."

"I'm so hungry I could eat a buffalo," Jessica said, sitting with her sister at the cafe near the pool for a late lunch. "How long ago did we order? An hour?"

"Only eight minutes," Elizabeth said, checking her watch. *If Jessica would wear a watch herself,* she thought, *she wouldn't have to ask everybody all the time.* "But I doubt this place serves buffalo. I'm sure they're a protected species on the island."

"Ha. Ha. I think we should have gone somewhere fancier for lunch. Dad said this whole trip is on him. I guess he feels guilty about Marin; we might as well take advantage of that while we can!"

Elizabeth gave her a disapproving glare but decided to let the remark slide. "You chose the restaurant," she reminded her sister. "You couldn't wait another minute for lunch, and this place was closest. But don't worry. We've got a whole week on the island to try other places to eat."

"We might be sitting here for the whole week!" Jessica complained. "Why are our salads taking so long? I bet Dad and Mom are eating somewhere chic and expensive after they finish their"—she laughed derisively—*"golf-cart tour!"*

Elizabeth took a sip of iced tea. "I think it's sweet that they wanted to take their own private tour."

"But by golf cart? That's totally tacky."

"You know that cars aren't allowed on the island," Elizabeth said. "How else would they get around?"

"Motorcycle?" Jessica suggested.

Elizabeth laughed. "Can't you just see Mom and Dad on a motorcycle?"

"In black leather, with studs," Jessica added archly. "Seriously, though, I was starting to worry

86

about the old parental units. They hardly talked to each other all last week! It was like living in an ice box with them around."

"I know," Elizabeth said thoughtfully. "I kept thinking about that time last year when they separated and thought about getting divorced. I've been so worried! All week it seemed like they haven't really been able to connect."

"I think Mom was mad that Dad didn't tell her about Marin," Jessica said.

"I can understand why she'd feel that way," Elizabeth said. "On the other hand, I guess Dad didn't want to scare her."

Jessica shrugged; other people's problems never concerned her for long. "It doesn't matter now," she said. "They seem OK together today."

"Yeah, they do. Did you notice them over by the pool? They looked happier together than they have in a long time. Younger, too. I'm glad they're going to spend some time alone together this week."

"Me, too!" Jessica declared. "Because if they're alone with each other, then they'll leave us alone. So we can do whatever we want!"

Elizabeth shook her head. "Your selflessness is inspiring," she said. "Anyhow, I think a private tour around the island could turn into a romantic afternoon for Mom and Dad, even on a golf cart. I hope when I've been married for twenty years, I'll still want to do romantic things alone with T—" She stopped herself, embarrassed, before the word "Todd" slipped out. "With my husband."

Jessica laughed. "You're so transparent, Liz. You almost said 'Todd,' didn't you?"

"No!" Elizabeth protested, feeling her face redden. She knew she was too young even to think about marriage to any one guy in particular, but sometimes it was tempting to imagine herself in her mother's wedding gown, floating down the aisle with flowers in her hair and Todd waiting for her at the front of a candlelit church, looking totally sexy in a tuxedo. *No*, she thought, *make that black tie and tails*.

Jessica grimaced. "You and Todd are so boring that it already seems like you've been married for thirty years."

A tall, skinny waitress appeared, with "Jill" on her name badge and unnatural red highlights in her hair. She set two salads down in front of the twins, and Jessica immediately dug into hers.

"After last week boring sounds pretty good to me," Elizabeth said, reaching for the oil and vinegar. "I let you talk me into looking for adventure then. Now I've learned my lesson. Get used to having plain old boring Liz back."

"Never!" Jessica said. "I'll just have to keep working at spicing up your life for you, since you're obviously incapable of doing it for yourself."

Elizabeth glared witheringly at her twin. "Gee, thanks," she said.

"You know what else is getting boring?" Jessica asked. "Dad's basket-case act. I can't put up with him spazzing out all week long, like he did at the pool a little while ago. I wanted to drown myself. Or him."

"I guess he's still uptight about Marin," Elizabeth said with a shrug.

"Did you see the way those two gorgeous hunks backed away from me when they saw that my father was an overprotective lunatic? This could be disastrous for my social life." Jessica shoved a huge leaf of lettuce into her mouth.

"Don't worry," Elizabeth told her sister. "I'm sure he'll relax in a day or two. And Mom said she'd keep him under control until then."

Jessica held out her glass for the skinny waitress to refill. "Let's do something awesome with the rest of the day, Liz. What do you think? Windsurfing? Parasailing?"

"Not me," Elizabeth said. "I don't want to expend that much energy. Besides, as I keep telling you, I'm not here for the excitement. I'm here to sightsee and relax."

"Horseback riding!" Jessica cried suddenly. "It's perfect! You can sit in the saddle and let the horse do all the work, while I watch for good-looking guys in tight jeans and boots. The best of both worlds!"

Elizabeth grinned over a forkful of tomato. "Actually, horseback riding sounds like fun," she said. "Let's run back to our room as soon as we've finished here and change out of our bathing suits."

Debbie Clayton leaned against the registration counter of the Hotel Orizaba. She was glad to be back at her usual spot at the front desk. Debbie had served drinks at the pool that afternoon only because she'd been filling in for another employee. It had meant a long day. But it was all part of being helpful to absolutely everyone, to convince management to choose her for employee of the month. That would look awesome on her application to hotel-management school.

And the hundred-dollar bonus she'd get as employee of the month would buy the new dress she'd been eyeing in the resort's boutique. It was sparkling white, with sequins around the low-cut neckline, and a short, swingy skirt that would twirl around her when she danced. She imagined the look on her fiancé's face when he saw her in it.

Debbie was saving up for school—and planning a wedding. Her mother's houseboat-rental service paid the bills and kept Debbie and her younger sisters fed and clothed, but it left no money for extras, including college.

In other words, every cent she made at the hotel was spent before she earned it. The only way she could afford a new dress was to be named employee of the month. And the only way she would win that honor was to be perky and upbeat and to give the customers everything they asked for.

As soon as she thought of customers, one appeared at the door, as if her musings had reeled him in. And what a customer! He was young, about twenty, with thick light-brown hair. He wore an oversize, tacky sweatshirt, with "Death Valley" printed across the front. But it couldn't hide his perfect, muscular body. His eyes were a deep, hypnotic blue.

"I need a room for the next few nights," the man said, flashing her a dazzling smile.

"Do you have a reservation?" she asked. "We're completely booked for this week."

He placed his elbows on the counter and gazed into her eyes. "No," he said, "I don't have a reservation. But you look as if you're a real expert at this job. You can figure out a way to help me, can't you?"

Debbie hesitated. The Avalon Suite had been left unreserved in case any VIPs showed up. But this guy didn't look like anyone important. He hadn't even brought any luggage with him.

"I don't want to get you in trouble or anything," the customer continued. "But it would sure make my day if you could find a room for me. Maybe a last-minute cancellation?"

Debbie turned to look behind her. Her manager was nowhere in sight. She punched a few keys on the computer. The Avalon Suite was still vacant.

"Well—" she began.

He smiled. "I could tell from the moment I saw you that you're the kind of employee who will do anything to serve a customer. I'll be sure to let the management know that you've been a great help."

The white sequined dress danced before Debbie's eyes. She glanced from the computer screen to the customer's handsome, friendly face. Then she smiled and whisked out one of the hotel's electronic door keys.

"As a matter of fact, we do have a cancellation," she said. "It's one of our nicest suites, though, so I'm afraid it's a little expensive—"

He pulled out a fat billfold. "Money's no object, but I have to pay you in cash. The airline lost my luggage, and I'm afraid all my credit cards were in my bag."

"What name is this under?" Debbie asked.

"LeShay. Leon LeShay."

"All right, Mr. LeShay, if you'll just sign here, I'll have you registered in a jiffy. We'll ring you if the airline comes by with your luggage. In the meantime you might need to buy a few items. The gift shop is just over there, to your left." She pointed. "And there's a boutique and a Western-wear shop on the other side of the courtyard, past the pool."

"Thanks so much," he said. "Somehow I knew you'd be a big help."

Debbie gave him her perkiest smile. "Is there anything else I can do for you, Mr. LeShay?"

The man smiled, and Debbie couldn't help noticing his amazingly white teeth. "Actually, there is," he said. "I'm here to see my friend Ned Wakefield. Could you tell me which room he's in?"

"I'm sorry," Debbie replied, "but I'm not allowed to give out that information. If you'd like, I can leave a message for him, saying that you're here."

"Oh, no!" the man said quickly. "I mean, I wouldn't want you to go through any trouble. But I'd sure like to know which room he's staying in. Of course, you've already been so helpful that I hate to ask for another favor—"

Debbie hesitated. Employees of the month did not ignore hotel policy. On the other hand, they didn't refuse customers a simple favor, either.

"Well, I guess that will be OK," she decided. "It's not as though you're an ax murderer or anything." She consulted her computer screen. "Mr. and Mrs. Wakefield are in room one-fourteen. Oh, no. That's wrong. That's their daughters' room. Ned and Alice are next door, in one-twelve."

"Thanks, Debbie," he said, reading her name badge. "You've been very helpful."

"My pleasure, sir," she answered. "And would you mind filling out this customer-comment card? There's a space on here for evaluating staff members who've given you especially good service."

He winked. "I'd love to."

*   *   *

Jessica loved being high off the ground on horseback, with a glossy mare named Black Beauty moving beneath her in response to the slightest pull on the reins. Even more than that, she loved watching Brad, the cute red-haired leader of the trip. He was riding a few feet ahead of her as he led a group of riders, mostly children, down a trail through the woods. *Some guys are built to wear jeans,* she decided.

Jessica had been disappointed to find that the guided horseback ride leaving at three o'clock consisted mostly of children, but having a good-looking guide made it all worthwhile. And being the only rider old enough to be interested in Brad— except Elizabeth, of course—meant that she had no competition for his attention.

She was glad she'd chosen to dress this way, she thought, glancing down at the teeny blue-and-white-striped bikini top and her ultrashort cutoffs. Of course, Elizabeth had tried to talk her into wearing jeans, saying her outfit wasn't practical for horseback riding. Not practical? That showed how much Elizabeth knew about it. It was totally practical for getting cute trail guides like Brad to notice her. She'd finally appeased her sister by taking a sweater, but she wore it tied around her waist, where it felt uncomfortably warm dangling over her hips.

"So, Brad, what does a guy like you do for fun around here?" she called up to him. "I mean, when you're not guiding kids through the woods on horses. There must be some really hot night spots on the island."

"Oh, there are a few," Brad said. "At night the cafe at the pool turns into a disco. We get pretty funky bands here. And there's a nightclub in Avalon—"

"I was thinking of places that are a little more private," Jessica interrupted, giving him a knowing glance. Out of the corner of her eye, she noticed Elizabeth pulling up beside her on a small but sturdy roan, shaking her head slightly. Jessica ignored her. It was just like Elizabeth to want to spoil her fun.

"Oh, I can think of a few spots," Brad said, watching her with budding interest. "The beach is beautiful at night. I know a secluded little cove that you would love."

"Hmmm. That does sound nice," Jessica murmured.

Suddenly Brad reined his horse and turned around. "Hey!" he called. At his sudden yell Jessica felt Black Beauty's powerful body jerk. She patted the mare's neck to steady her. Brad was pointing at the rear of the column of riders. Two of the riders, both about nine years old, were coaxing their ponies off the trail, into the woods.

"Excuse me, Jessica," Brad said with an apologetic tip of his cowboy hat. "Duty calls." He raised his voice again. "Billy and Tiffany, I told you to stay on the trail!" He rode back along the line of riders, calling, "All riders must remain on the trail at all times!"

As soon as he was gone, Elizabeth reined her roan up close to Jessica's mare. Jessica looked down at her from her larger horse.

Unlike her sister, Elizabeth had changed out of her bathing suit. She was wearing a striped orange-and-white top and a pair of loose khaki walking shorts. Her outfit reminded Jessica of one of those orange Creamsicles from the elementary-school cafeterias. *Leave it to Liz to dress like something so . . . juvenile,* she thought. To Jessica's disgust Elizabeth had wanted to wear long pants for horse-back riding, but Jessica had convinced her that the day was too hot.

"What do you think you're doing?" Elizabeth asked, tugging at the neckline of her top as if trying to fan some air against her skin. The air had grown oppressively warm as they'd traveled deeper into the woods, and Elizabeth was sweating.

Jessica shrugged. "I'm sitting on a horse, waiting for our guide to come back, same as you."

"You're flirting with a guy who's a complete stranger!"

"So?" Jessica asked. "What's the big deal?"

"I can't see why you'd want to get involved with a strange man," Elizabeth said. "After what happened last week."

"Who said I was getting involved?" Jessica

protested. "We're only talking—not eloping!"

Elizabeth shook her head again. "Sometimes I just don't understand you."

"Why are you in such a crummy mood?" her twin asked. "Aren't you having a good time?"

"No," Elizabeth answered. "I wish we had waited to go horseback riding tomorrow. These kids are so slow!"

"I thought you liked kids!"

"I do, but I'm sick of walking my horse; I want to canter. Look up ahead on the trail." Elizabeth pointed to a spot in the distance. "See that place in the distance, where the big tree branch reaches across? I'll race you to it."

Jessica shook her head. "I don't think so. Brad said we were supposed to stay together."

"I know," Elizabeth admitted. "But it's hot and stuffy here. I want to feel the wind blowing by me. Brad won't mind, as long as we stay in sight. The trail's perfectly straight. He'll be able to see us the whole way. We can wait for him and the others up ahead."

Jessica was tempted to go with her. The slow pace made the riding less exciting than she had hoped. Still, Brad looked awfully exciting in those blue jeans of his.

"You go ahead," she decided. "I'll wait for the others."

Elizabeth felt wings of hair breaking free from her ponytail as the wind rushed by. Her whole body jolted violently as she bounced on top of her reddish horse, named, inexplicably, Fred. Then the jolting stopped as Fred's trot smoothed into a gallop. The trees along the trail blended together, like a watercolor painting in browns and greens. And Elizabeth sailed along, no longer feeling the horse's feet as they hit the ground.

"This is exactly what I needed," she called into the wind. The conversation with Jessica had made her think again of how foolish she had been to fall for John Marin. It was dangerous to let her heart go like that. From now on, she decided, she would lead with her head—beginning as soon as she finished her horseback ride.

For now, it was the horse's head that was leading. And Elizabeth's troubles seemed to fly away behind her as she galloped down the quiet trail alone.

Jill Reese lay on a lounge chair by the pool, wondering if her bathing suit made her look as flat-chested as she thought it did. Occasionally a guy flirted with her while she was waiting tables—while she was dressed in real clothes. But as soon as she got off waitress duty and into her swimsuit, they stayed away as if she were poison. *What good are free pool passes for employees,* Jill wondered, *if they're the only kind of passes I ever get?*

She looked around at all the women and teenage girls with beautiful, curvy figures. She wasn't asking to be transformed into Dolly Parton. A nice, slender figure like the ones on those pretty blond twins at the cafe this afternoon—now, that would be a definite improvement. They were probably about a size six, like her. But not so tall and gangly. And unlike her, they were perfectly proportioned—even on top.

Suddenly she saw a man walking toward her. She pulled off her sunglasses. This couldn't be happening. He was the best-looking guy she'd seen all day—about twenty years old, with light-brown hair and a great body. And he really was walking directly toward her. She couldn't believe it. Her luck was finally turning.

"Hi!" he called, pulling up a chair next to hers.

Jill thought she might faint.

"You work here, don't you?" he asked.

"Does it show?"

He laughed, and she saw that he had the brightest, straightest, most beautiful teeth she had ever seen. "I saw you waiting tables a little while ago."

"That was me, all right," Jill said. "It's not glamorous, but it pays my tuition."

"I thought maybe you could help me with something," he said. "I noticed two girls eating a late lunch at the cafe this afternoon. I think you waited on them."

Jill sighed. She seemed destined to be the girl every guy talked to for advice about how to get the girl he really wanted. "I doubt I can help you," she admitted. "I waited on dozens of customers this afternoon. I'm sure I wouldn't remember who you mean."

"Oh, I think you'd remember these two," he said. "They're about sixteen years old, blond, and absolutely identical. They look like they stepped out of a Doublemint-gum commercial."

"Oh, sure," Jill said. "The Doublemint twins. I remember them. One grilled-tuna salad, one avo-cado-and-citrus."

"That's them," he said. "Did they say where they were heading this afternoon? It's important that I talk to them."

Jill considered telling him she had no idea where the twins were, but that he could stick around and talk to her for as long as he wanted. But she was an employee. And employees were supposed to think of the hotel guests first.

"Actually, I did hear them make plans for the afternoon," she told him reluctantly. "They said they were going horseback riding."

"You were right," Jessica said glumly as she joined Elizabeth at the place where the tree branch hung over the trail. She had followed her sister only a few minutes later. "It is dangerous to flirt with strange men."

Elizabeth's eyes widened. "What happened? Are you all right?"

"Brad is *married*!" Jessica exclaimed. "Can you believe it? And the jerk was coming on to me."

Elizabeth looked relieved. "From my viewpoint it looked like it was you who was doing most of the coming on."

"Well, he wasn't exactly discouraging it," Jessica shot back. "If that whiny pipsqueak Tiffany hadn't let it slip about meeting his wife at the stable yesterday—"

"It's a good thing she did let it slip," Elizabeth said.

Brad and the other riders caught up to them, and the twins fell in line in the middle of the group.

"I can see why you wanted to go faster," Jessica said. "The slow pace is getting to me, too. And all these little brats are bringing back horrible memories of my spring break as a camp counselor. Let's leave Brad and his kiddies behind and set off to do some exploring for ourselves."

"You know we can't do that," Elizabeth said.

"Why not?" Jessica asked. "You did it yourself, just a little while ago."

"That was different. I stayed where Brad could see me. You're talking about going off on our own for the rest of the trip."

"I don't see what difference it makes," Jessica said.

"The rules say we have to stay on the trail with the group," Elizabeth lectured.

"So?" Jessica shrugged. "Rules were meant to be broken."

"That's what people always say when they want to do things they shouldn't do."

"Liz, what would the world be like if we all did what we were supposed to do?" She searched her brain for some names that would impress her intellectual sister. "Galileo broke the rules. So did Marie Curie and, uh . . . Susan B. Anthony."

"It's not the same thing," Elizabeth said uncertainly.

"Sure it is. Besides, you said you were fed up with going so slow. Let's ask Brad," Jessica suggested, suddenly inspired. "He's in charge here. If he says we can, then we're not doing anything that's against the rules. OK?"

Elizabeth smiled. "I guess it's worth a try."

They caught up with Brad at the head of the line and made their proposal.

"I don't know, girls," he said. "It's against the rules to go off trail."

Elizabeth shot Jessica an I-told-you-so glance.

"Come on, Brad," Jessica pleaded. "You know we're good riders. Besides, we won't just plow into the woods with no direction. I see a side trail up ahead, to the right. Let us turn onto that one and do some exploring on our own."

"I don't like the idea," Brad said. "We're about to get into some rocky, hilly country. The trails twist around a lot, and some of the minor ones are overgrown. It can be hard to find your way. What if you get lost?"

"All these trails lead back to the stables eventually, don't they?" Jessica asked.

"Well, yes, they do," Brad admitted.

"So as long as we stick to a trail—any trail—we'll get back," Jessica said.

"I'm still not crazy about the idea of you kids riding around in the woods by yourself. It's almost quarter to five already. I don't want to have to come back tonight to lead the search party if you get lost."

Jessica injected just the right amount of ice into her tone. "I can see why you wouldn't want to do that," she said slowly. "After all, your *wife* would probably be waiting for you at home."

Brad gulped, and Jessica knew she had scored.

"All right!" Brad said finally. "Go ahead. But if anyone asks, you slipped away without telling me."

Mr. Wakefield let go of his wife's hand as they entered the hotel lobby at five o'clock Saturday afternoon. "There's the gift shop," he said, pointing. "I'm sure you can buy your postcards in there."

Mrs. Wakefield kissed him on the cheek. "Today has been wonderful," she said. "I never thought a golf cart could go that fast!"

He laughed. "Only if you don't mind breaking the laws of physics!"

"Next time," she promised, "we'll rent two golf carts, and I'll race you."

"You're on! But we'd better make sure the girls have enough cash to bail us out of jail for traffic violations."

"I'm not worried," Mrs. Wakefield said, grabbing on to her husband's arm. "I know a great attorney."

Mrs. Wakefield began pulling him toward the gift shop, but he pointed to the registration desk. "I left the room key with the front-desk clerk," he said. "I'll go get it and check our messages, and then I'll meet you in the shop in a few minutes."

His wife kissed him lightly on the lips as they parted.

Mr. Wakefield sauntered over to the front counter, chuckling at the memory of his wife's face as he'd floored the accelerator on the golf cart. He was sure he'd been smiling nonstop for two hours. Finally he was at peace. The afternoon had been fun and carefree, and he was more in love with his wife than ever before. The horror of the last two weeks no longer lurked around every corner of his mind, waiting to jump out and grab him off guard.

He waved at the front-desk clerk, whose name badge said "Debbie." "You certainly get around," he said in a jovial tone. "Didn't you serve us drinks at the pool today?"

"I sure did, Mr. Wakefield," she said in the bouncy, perky way of young service workers trying too hard to make a good impression. "I was filling in for a friend. This is my real job."

"I need to pick up my room key," Mr. Wakefield told her. "Are there any messages? It's room one-twelve."

Debbie checked the box. "Yep, here's one. It's from your daughters."

He unfolded the slip of paper she handed him. "Mom and Dad," began Elizabeth's precise script. "We hope you're having a good day. We're going horseback riding this afternoon. We'll see you at dinner. Love, Liz and Jess."

"Thanks," he said to Debbie. He turned around to go meet Alice in the gift shop, but Debbie stopped him.

"Actually," she said, "you did have another message. Well, sort of. He didn't leave anything written, but a friend of yours came by this afternoon. He said you didn't know he was staying here."

Mr. Wakefield heard a rushing sound in his ears. "A friend?"

"That's right," Debbie continued, oblivious to his distress. "He had light-brown hair and dark-blue eyes. About your height, but with really broad shoulders."

With every word Mr. Wakefield felt his face draining of blood. The description fit John Marin. "But that's impossible!" he blurted out.

Debbie looked at him curiously. "Excuse me? Is something wrong, Mr. Wakefield?"

He turned to her, his eyes blazing. "Did my, uh, *friend* leave a name?"

Debbie keyed a few characters into her computer. "Yes, sir. His name is Leon LeShay." Suddenly she looked frightened. "You do know him, don't you?"

"Yes, I know him, all right," he said, troubled. The description sounded like Marin, but the alias didn't seem like something Marin would use. Mr. Wakefield took a deep breath. Then he turned and stalked out of the lobby, forgetting until he reached room 112 that he was supposed to meet his wife.

"Tony?" he yelled into the phone a few minutes later, after Detective Cabrini picked up the line at the Sweet Valley police station. "It's Ned Wakefield." He crossed his fingers tightly.

"Ned!" Cabrini's voice sounded frantic. "Thank goodness you got my messages. I'm glad you're safe."

"Messages? What messages? What's happened?"

"You don't know?" Tony asked, sounding worried.

A horrible premonition came over Mr. Wakefield. *No!* he told himself. *It can't be.* He raised his voice without realizing it. "*What* don't I know?"

Cabrini took a deep breath. "John Marin is free. He escaped from prison this morning."

"*What do you mean, he escaped from prison?*" the attorney yelled into the receiver as his world crashed into splinters around him—like the window of Elizabeth's bedroom the night Marin had smashed through it.

106

"Marin killed one prison guard," Cabrini said. "He kidnapped another guard, and she still hasn't been found. The warden's afraid she could be dead, too."

"Do you have any leads?" Mr. Wakefield asked flatly.

"Sort of," Cabrini said. "We think Marin carjacked a station wagon in the desert, from a family of tourists from Utah. He must be heading south—probably to the border."

"The border? Yeah, right," Mr. Wakefield said, not believing it for an instant. "Dammit, Tony! You know as well as I do where he's headed. Marin's obsessed with my family. I know how this guy thinks. And I know he'd make a beeline straight for my daughters."

"Ned, don't jump to conclusions—"

"Tony, he might be here already!" Mr. Wakefield startled himself with the shrill edge of panic in his own voice.

"I doubt that," Cabrini said, trying to be reasonable. "He only just broke out of prison today. Even if he is coming after your family, it would take him a few days to track you down. He has no way of knowing where you are."

"Then why did a man who fits Marin's description tell the front-desk clerk that he's my friend?" Mr. Wakefield asked.

"Calm down, Ned," Cabrini told him. "A lot of people fit Marin's description."

"A lot of people didn't try to murder my daughters!"

"Try to stay calm," the detective urged. "I'll alert the police force there on the island. And I'll get the coast guard involved too, to catch him as he crosses the channel. Damn! I wish we could locate that missing prison guard. If LeShay is still alive, she could probably tell us a lot."

Mr. Wakefield froze. "Who?"

"Leighann LeShay. She's the prison guard Marin kidnapped."

Leighann LeShay? The "friend" at the front desk had given his name as *Leon* LeShay. Mr. Wakefield gasped, feeling as if he were drowning in a nightmare. None of this was real. It couldn't be.

"Ned? Ned!" came Cabrini's voice through the phone. "Are you still there? What's wrong?"

Mr. Wakefield shook his head, his eyes closed. "Forget about contacting the coast guard," he choked out. "It's too late for that. Marin is already on the island."

Chapter 7

Behind the stable, Joe Garcia leaned his chair back against the wall and lit up a Lucky Strike. He'd promised his fiancée, Debbie, that he would quit smoking, and he had almost managed it—he was down to only one cigarette a day. But that one cigarette was proving to be the hardest one to give up. Joe's five o'clock smoke was more than a cigarette. It was a ritual.

He gazed into the peaceful forest, where smoky shadows were beginning to gather beneath the trees. Almost everybody thought the view from the front of the stable was more spectacular—with the red-tile roof of the hotel glinting in the sun, and a trace of ocean visible in the distance. But to Joe's mind it was a tourist's view. Out here, behind the stable, was a Catalina most tourists never saw. No hype. No picture-postcard views. Just hills and trees and pure serenity.

Five o'clock was Joe's favorite time of day in the summer. His afternoon chores were finished, and he had a good twenty minutes before any of the groups who were out horseback riding started trickling back. He'd have plenty of work to do then, until six, when the three o'clock group was due to return. But for now Joe was alone, with some time to think.

Today he had to think about Debbie's twenty-second birthday. She'd been dying to buy a party dress she'd seen in the resort's boutique. Joe didn't know much about women's clothes, but he thought the white flowing dress would look really sexy with Debbie's dark hair and ruby lipstick. He'd like nothing more than to buy Debbie that dress and celebrate her birthday by taking her to Villa Portofino for dinner and then over to the Avalon Casino for some hot dancing.

Joe sighed. The front legs of his chair landed in the dirt with a soft thump, and he poked at his glasses to push them back into place. This view of the forest always worked miracles for his mood. But it couldn't work miracles for his wallet. He couldn't afford to buy Debbie that dress, or to take her out for a special evening. They would have to settle for blue jeans and Mexican food, like last year.

A horse whinnied. Joe jumped up, surprised to hear footsteps on the wooden-plank sidewalk. It was too early for one of the guided tours to be returning. He crushed the rest of his Lucky Strike into the dirt and sauntered around the building to see who was interrupting his daily meditations.

"Howdy!" called a well-built man with sandy-brown hair and a big grin. "My name's Leon. What does a guy have to do to rent a horse around here?"

Joe smiled apologetically. "I'm sorry, but you'll have to come back tomorrow. Our last guided horseback ride of the day left at three o'clock."

"That's OK," the man said. "I'm an experienced rider, and I know the island. I don't need a guide."

"Sorry," Joe repeated, trying to keep his tone friendly and polite—since, after all, this was a hotel guest. "But I'm not allowed to go against hotel policy. I can't let you take out a horse without a guide, no matter how qualified a rider you are."

Leon pulled a billfold from his jeans and began unfolding twenty-dollar bills. "I sure would like to take out a horse this afternoon," he said quietly. "Would a hundred dollars cover your trouble?"

Joe gulped. A hundred dollars would buy that white dress Debbie was in love with. He glanced at the sky. There were still several hours of sunlight left. But what if Leon wasn't as good a rider as he claimed? What if there was an accident? Or what if Joe's boss showed up and asked about the missing horse?

Joe peered into the stable, thinking fast. His boss almost never came by this late in the day. And if he chose the oldest, safest horse in the stable, surely Leon wouldn't get into any trouble. There was Old Lacey in her stall, watching them calmly from her big brown eyes. She'd be perfect.

"OK, sir," Joe said finally. "You've got a deal. You can take out Old Lacey; she's as gentle as a kitten. Just have her in by dark—and remember that the sun goes down behind the mountains early on this part of the island, even in June. And it may storm tonight, so it could get dark sooner than usual. Don't stay out late."

"Don't worry," Leon said, smiling. "This shouldn't take too long."

Mrs. Wakefield pushed open the door to room 112.

"Ned?" she asked as her eyes adjusted to the dimness. Outside, the late-afternoon sun had been bright. But inside the room the shades were drawn, and her husband hadn't bothered to turn on a light. "I thought you were going to meet me in the gift shop. The clerk at the front desk told me the girls went horseback riding."

Mr. Wakefield sat on the bed, with his back to his wife and his posture rigid. "All right," he said. "You call the police, and I'll find the girls."

"What in the world are you talking about?" Mrs. Wakefield asked. Then she noticed that he had spoken into the telephone receiver in his hand. "Ned? *What's wrong?*"

"Yes," said her husband. "I'll call if I get any leads. And call me the minute you know anything. If you can't find me, leave a message at the desk."

Mrs. Wakefield heard something crackle under her foot. A folded sheet of paper was on the floor. Obviously it had been slipped under the door. "What's this?" she asked absentmindedly. She picked up the sheet of paper just as her husband slammed the telephone receiver into its cradle.

He whirled to face her, his expression grim. "John Marin escaped from prison this morning," he said. "And he's here on Catalina."

His wife sat down limply on the bed. "Are you sure?" she whispered. She nervously tore off a corner of the paper in her hand.

He nodded, his eyes full of fear.

Mrs. Wakefield's gaze dropped to her lap, and she suddenly caught sight of the words scrawled in large, angular letters on the sheet of Hotel Orizaba stationery. "Oh, Ned!" she cried. "Look at this!"

She handed him the sheet of paper and saw her own horror reflected in his eyes. *"Horseback riding can be dangerous, Counselor,"* the note said. It was signed *"JM."*

Elizabeth coaxed her horse alongside her sister's. High up on Black Beauty, Jessica stared around her as if perplexed. Wooded hills had given way to a rocky, rugged landscape. The trees were spaced farther apart now, and interspersed with exotic, glossy-leaved vegetation and tall, stubby, cactuslike plants that left long shadows in the light of late afternoon. Elizabeth followed her sister's gaze to the unmarked ground in front of them, where patches of pine needles lay undisturbed in the sand.

Elizabeth felt her annoyance rising. "What happened to the trail you were supposed to be following?" she asked sharply.

"I have no idea," Jessica said. "It just sort of disappeared a while back."

"Then why didn't you turn around?" Elizabeth asked. "You were in the lead. It was your turn to navigate!"

"I kept thinking we were on a part of the trail that's gotten overgrown," Jessica explained. "I figured we'd hit a real trail again soon."

Elizabeth sighed. "Now we don't even have any idea what direction we came from," she said. "We've probably been traveling in circles. I can't believe I let you get us lost!"

"We're not really lost," Jessica insisted brightly. "We know we're in the woods. And we know we're still on Catalina Island—"

"Do you rehearse your lame comments ahead of time," Elizabeth asked, "or do you improvise on the spot?"

Jessica glared at her twin. "Why do you always

have to get sarcastic when we run into a little bitty problem?" Her voice rose to a high pitch, and Black Beauty, who'd seemed skittish all afternoon, did a nervous dance until Jessica reined her in. "I hate it when you get sarcastic!" she concluded.

"And I hate it when you get us into trouble!" Elizabeth responded. "Leaving the group was your idea, remember?"

"Nobody twisted your arm to follow me!"

Elizabeth sighed. "Well," she said, "somebody had to look after you, since you're obviously incapable of looking after yourself."

"Right. And I can see what a good job you've done of it!" Jessica said, gesturing toward their rugged, unfamiliar surroundings. "Thanks for looking out for me, *big* sister. What would I ever do without you? I swear, Liz, you have no right to act like you're the boss, just because you're four minutes older than me—"

"This has nothing to do with age," Elizabeth argued. "It has to do with common sense!"

Jessica put her hands on her hips, and her eyes blazed. "If you have so much common sense," she said icily, "then why are you lost in the middle of the woods, screaming your lungs out, sitting on a horse with an idiotic name like Fred?"

Elizabeth was too frustrated to answer and instead let out an exasperated groan. Besides, Jessica had a point. Deep down, Elizabeth knew she had to take her share of the blame for getting lost.

Anyhow, arguing was accomplishing nothing. "Leave Fred out of this," she said. "It's not his fault." She nudged Fred in the flanks with her left sneaker, to turn him away from Jessica and Black Beauty.

Peering into the trees, Elizabeth didn't understand how it could be growing so dark so quickly. She checked her watch. It wasn't even five thirty. But birdsong had been replaced by the repetitive chirp of crickets, and the temperature was dropping rapidly, though it had seemed hot just a half hour earlier. Elizabeth was wearing only a short-sleeved top, and goose pimples were already poking out on her bare arms. Of course, Jessica was wearing a bikini top that was much skimpier. But at least Jessica had a sweater tied around her waist.

"Gee, it's getting dark," Jessica said suddenly. "How did it get so late, so fast?"

"I don't know," Elizabeth said, double-checking her watch. "It's not late enough to be so dark, in June."

"Maybe it's an eclipse," Jessica suggested.

"Maybe your brain is eclipsed," Elizabeth responded distractedly.

Suddenly Elizabeth knew one reason why night seemed to be falling so early. The twins had been traveling around the outskirts of one of the island's rocky peaks, which now jutted up sharply between them and the afternoon sun. On top of the summit, a few trees waved wildly in the gathering wind.

116

"Do you recognize that peak?" Elizabeth asked. "If we can remember seeing it from the hotel, we might be able to get an idea of where we are."

Jessica shook her head. "Nope. It looks like a mound of rocks and trees to me, like all the other mounds of rocks and trees."

"I don't recognize it either." Elizabeth sighed, feeling helpless. In another couple hours it would be completely dark. And they had no idea which direction led to the hotel and their parents.

"Well, we can't be *that* lost," Jessica offered. "It's not that big an island."

Elizabeth scowled. Jessica was legendary for having no sense of direction. *Unless I figure a way out of this,* Elizabeth thought, *we'll be lost in the wilderness at night, alone.*

Brad sighed, glad that he was finally heading back to the stables with this last riding group of the day. Groups made up of mostly kids were always the hardest ones to lead. "Get down, Billy!" he yelled to a towheaded nine-year-old on a coal-black pony in the middle of the line. "We don't try to stand up when we're on a pony's back."

"I want to be in the circus!" Billy announced.

"Can I be in the circus, too?" asked Tiffany, whose pony plodded along right behind Brad's horse.

"You already *are* in the circus," Brad said. "This whole trip is a circus!" He shook his head. These little kids were driving him crazy. The only riders in this group who were over the age of twelve had been those pretty teenage twins—the ones who had stupidly insisted on going off on their own. He never should have given in and let them go. But when Jessica had brought up his wife like that— well, it had caught him off guard.

He hoped the twins hadn't got into any trouble. Sure, both girls were decent riders. But they didn't know the landscape. If they got lost or hurt, Brad knew that he'd probably lose his job at the resort.

"Who's that man?" Tiffany asked, pointing at the trail up ahead as they rounded a bend.

About ten yards away a tall, well-built man who looked a little younger than Brad sat astride Old Lacey. The man was digging his heels impatiently into the mare's dirty white flanks. "Come on, you lazy nag!" the man urged. Old Lacey, engrossed in munching vegetation by the side of the trail, calmly ignored him.

Brad frowned. "I don't know who he is," he said in a low voice. "I've never seen him before. But nobody is supposed to take out a horse without a guide. I wonder what he's up to." Then he realized he was talking to a nine-year-old. "He's just a man who's trying to get the horse to go," Brad told her. "Lacey can be pretty stubborn."

Tiffany appraised the stranger. "He's cuter than you," she told Brad.

Brad rolled his eyes. "Excuse me, sir," he

called. He tried to keep his voice polite, in case the man was a hotel guest. "Can I help you with something?"

The stranger looked up quickly. His dark-blue eyes widened with surprise, and he visibly struggled to control his frustration. When he spoke, his voice was calm and friendly. "I'm just having a heck of a time getting this old mare to move into those trees."

"There's a good reason for that," Brad said, dismounting. "Lacey is one of our oldest trail horses. And trail horses are trained to stay on the trail."

"Those two teenagers were on trail horses, and they didn't stay on the trail," Tiffany said.

"Well, some trail horses are more obedient than others," Brad said, wishing he were at home in his reclining chair, watching a baseball game on television. "And the twins did stay on the trail—they just took a different route." Brad turned to face the rest of the group. "You kids stop right where you are and wait for me!" he called.

"What twins?" the stranger asked. For an instant something about his face frightened Brad. The man's wide, easy smile seemed amused, but his eyes were glittering coldly. Brad blinked his own eyes, and the man's face returned to normal. *It must have been the late-afternoon sun in the trees,* he decided.

"There were two bee-yoo-ti-ful teenagers with long yellow hair," Tiffany explained. "But they

119

were mean. They said we were too slow, but we weren't! They went away, over that way," she added, pointing.

"Two gorgeous blondes, huh?" the stranger asked Brad with a companionable wink. "And you let them get away?"

"I didn't have any choice," Brad replied, thinking ruefully of Jessica's low-cut bathing-suit top and long legs. "They found out about my wife."

Tiffany giggled.

"Tiffany, you go back to the other kids," Brad said. "I mean now!" He was annoyed with the little brat, but he was also feeling nervous around the good-looking young man who hadn't offered his name. The stranger seemed harmless enough, for a greenhorn without a lot of horse sense. Still, Brad was responsible for the children's safety; he wasn't supposed to let them talk to strangers while on these trips.

Tiffany didn't move. "Can I get off my horsey, too?"

"No, you can't," he told the little girl. "Go back to the other kids, like I said. And be quiet! This will only take me a minute. Now go!"

Pouting, Tiffany turned her pony around and walked it back to the other children.

"Are you one of the Orizaba's trail guides?" the stranger asked. His voice was casual, but his eyes were intense.

"Yes, sir," Brad answered.

"Then maybe you can tell me what I'm doing wrong." The man gestured helplessly at Old Lacey. "How do I get this nag to gallop?"

"Gallop?" Brad asked. "You've got a better chance of getting a wooden carousel horse to gallop. Old Lacey is the slowest, steadiest horse on this island."

"At this point I'd settle for walking," the young man said ruefully.

"Walking, she'll do," Brad said. "But not in that direction. I told you, Lacey won't go off the trail. Not for you. Not for me. Not for anyone."

"Are all the horses around here like that?" the man asked.

Brad laughed. "Most are, but not all." He patted his own mahogany-colored mount. "For instance, Big Red here is the best off-trail horse around."

"I'm sorry, sir," Joe told the frantic middle-aged man. "But hotel guests aren't allowed to take a horse out without a guide."

"So get me a guide!" the dark-haired man insisted.

"There aren't any," Joe told him. "Only one guide is still on duty this late, and he's out with a group of riders."

"Then let me go by myself!" The man's hands trembled as he pleaded with Joe. "I only need a couple of hours. It's a matter of life and death!"

Joe chuckled inwardly. Guests of the resort were a pampered, self-centered bunch. Rich guys like this one considered pretty much everything to be a matter of life and death—from a stock-market slump to a shortage of airplane seats in first class. "I'd like to help you, sir, but the rules—"

"I'll pay you!" the man practically screamed. He yanked his wallet from his pocket and thumbed through it. He shoved a bill at Joe.

"Fifty dollars?" Joe asked, incredulous. He wondered if there was a full moon that night— *something* was making the guests freak out. Only a lunatic would pay fifty dollars to borrow a broken-down old trail horse for two hours. And the last crazy guest, Leon, had given him twice that. Leon's hundred dollars would be enough to buy Debbie's dress. This fifty dollars would go a long way toward a nice dinner.

"I'll pay you a hundred dollars!" the guest cried, pulling out another bill. "It's all I have with me."

"One hundred dollars?" Joe repeated. *Dinner, drinks, and dancing,* he thought happily. *Plus a corsage.*

Joe accepted the money. "All right, mister, you've got yourself a horse. But be sure to have her back by sunset."

Mr. Wakefield shifted from one foot to the other as the young stable hand took his time sad-dling up a horse. The horse was large, a gray gelding with white speckles. The stable guy had called it Satchmo. The twins' father didn't care what color the horse was or what its name was, and he didn't want to hear Joe's mindless patter about why Western saddles were better than English ones. He just wanted to get onto the horse and go out after his daughters.

His wife had begged him to wait in the hotel room until the authorities arrived, but every minute counted. Elizabeth and Jessica were out in those woods, and John Marin was on the loose. When Mrs. Wakefield had seen that his mind was made up, she had wanted to come, too. He had asked her to stay behind and start throwing together their belongings, so the family could leave the island as soon as he returned with the twins. Besides, somebody would have to talk to the police when they arrived.

"This is beginning to feel like déjà vu all over again, if you know what I mean," the stable hand commented as he handed Mr. Wakefield the reins. "I guess it's just my lucky day."

The counselor whirled around to glare at the stable hand. "What do you mean?"

"It's the darnedest thing," the younger man explained. "But can you believe that you're the second hotel guest in here this afternoon desperate to rent a horse at any price?"

"Who else was here?" Mr. Wakefield demanded. "Tell me!"

The man's eyes widened. "I know it was against the rules, but he offered me a hundred dollars, just like you did, and—"

"Who was he?" Mr. Wakefield thundered.

"His name was Leon something-or-other," the stable hand said, surprised at Mr. Wakefield's intensity. "He was about your height, with light-brown hair."

John Marin.

Icy fear gripped Mr. Wakefield's heart. He swung his body onto the horse's back and cantered away from the astonished stable hand, racing headlong toward the gloom beneath the trees.

Brad sighed gratefully as the trail rounded a bend near a huge old pine tree. The stable was only a few minutes away. This terrible last ride of the day would soon be over. He plodded along on Old Lacey, longing for his usual mount's sprightly step and quick reflexes.

"I liked your reddish-brownish horse better," Tiffany said, riding up alongside him.

Brad narrowed his eyes. He liked Big Red better, too. But he wasn't about to admit that to a nine-year-old. "Get back in line!" he ordered.

"Why did you and that cute guy trade horses?" the girl asked.

"None of your business!" Brad snapped.

But the question was a valid one. Brad couldn't believe he'd let the guy talk him into trading horses. One minute they'd been standing there chatting about the stubbornness of trail horses. The next minute the man with the dark-blue eyes was swinging his lean, muscular body into Big Red's saddle, while Brad mounted tired Old Lacey.

He wished he had the stranger's persuasive powers. They might have worked wonders with pretty, blond Jessica of the low-cut bikini top and long legs.

Jessica swatted a mosquito, but not until after it had raised a red welt on her thigh. She wished she hadn't insisted on wearing shorts. At least the wind was picking up. It felt cold against her bare legs, but it might help blow the mosquitoes away. "Whose idea was horseback riding, anyway?" she asked.

Elizabeth glowered at her. "Yours."

"Oh." They plodded on in silence for a few minutes, and Jessica noticed how dark it was getting. As usual, she wasn't wearing a watch, but she guessed that she and her sister had been lost for a good two hours. "I guess we never should have left the group."

"That's a blinding flash of the obvious," Elizabeth replied evenly.

Something loomed up ahead of them. *"Liz! What's that?"* Jessica shouted.

"It's only one of those cactuslike things," Elizabeth said. Her face was calm, but Jessica heard a tremor in her voice. "They're all over the place."

For the first time Jessica noticed that they really weren't riding through woods anymore. "You're right. Those cactus things are everywhere. And the ground is almost all rock. We seem to be going up. Are we climbing a mountain?"

"I don't think so," Elizabeth said in an impatient voice. "I think we're close to the shoreline."

"How can we be close to the shoreline?" Jessica asked. "It doesn't look like any beach *I've* ever seen. I bet the shore is miles from here. Admit it, Liz. You don't have any idea where we are."

"Fine," Elizabeth said. "If you know this island so well, then *you* figure out which way to go—the same way you figured out how to get us lost!"

Jessica pouted. "You're impossible!"

"Then it must run in the family," Elizabeth shot back.

Jessica suddenly reined in Black Beauty and stiffened, listening. "What's that noise?" she asked.

Elizabeth smiled triumphantly. "It sounds like the ocean to me. But I guess it couldn't be. Remember, the shore is miles from here."

Jessica glared at her twin and started Black Beauty into motion. "You think you're so smart," she muttered dangerously.

"I never said that," her sister protested. "All I said was—"

Suddenly the horses stepped out onto a flat

126

rock ledge. For a moment Jessica felt as if she were on top of the Empire State Building. Her horse shied. "Whoa, Black Beauty!" she called.

The twins reeled at the unexpected vista that stretched out in front of and below them. Their long, misshapen shadows fell over the edge of the high cliff. Far below, the pounding waves of the Pacific Ocean threatened to engulf a narrow strip of creamy beach and jagged gray rocks. The water was a deep midnight-blue under an overcast sky. The only signs of life were a few ash-colored seagulls wheeling overhead.

Jessica sighed miserably. They were close to the beach, all right. But it was a totally undeveloped, uninhabited beach. And it was a good eighty feet below them, at the bottom of the cliff.

"What do we now?" Jessica asked in a small voice. She was still mad at Elizabeth. But almost instinctively, she trusted her twin to solve their problems.

Elizabeth's face looked pale, and Jessica realized that her sister was very tired. "I think I have some idea where we are now," Elizabeth said in a resigned voice. She gestured toward the sweep of coastline to the north. "If we continue along the coast in that direction, we'll get to a campground I saw on the map, right off the beach. There's a road leading from that campground to our hotel."

"So all we have to do is follow the beach, and we'll get back to civilization?" Jessica asked.

"I think so," Elizabeth replied.

"But we're way up here on a cliff!" Jessica said worriedly. "How do we get down to the beach?"

"This is the highest point," Elizabeth said. "The cliffs start sloping downward as soon as we start going north. If we follow the path along the rim of the cliffs, it should bring us down to the level of the beach. Eventually."

Jessica peered around from the top of Black Beauty. "I don't see any path!" she cried.

"It's right there," Elizabeth said, pointing to a narrow track off to one side.

Jessica's eyes widened. Now she could see the stony path leading down from the outcropping they were on. But it was overgrown and littered with rocks that had fallen from higher elevations. Even worse, the path was only a couple feet wide at some points, and it fell off sharply on the left side, revealing a straight drop down to jagged rocks peppered by ocean spray.

Jessica took a deep breath. She had got them into this. She would get them out. "I'll lead the way," she said. "Follow me."

Mr. Wakefield squinted to make out the dial of his watch. It was only seven thirty—the sun couldn't have set yet. But shadows clustered thickly under the trees, distorting the shapes and colors of everything around him. And he still had found no sign of the twins.

"Elizabeth!" he called. "Jessica!"

The only response was the faint echo of his own voice, bouncing off some distant rocky hillside.

He gripped the gray gelding's flanks tightly with his calves. "Come on, Satchmo," he whispered, feeling very small in the rugged, unfamiliar landscape. Danger seemed to lurk behind every tree, and he expected to see John Marin riding out of the shadows at any moment.

He shuddered at the thought of Marin's cold, vengeance-filled eyes. But he wished that the murderer would appear before him. If Marin was here, with him, then at least Mr. Wakefield could be sure the killer wasn't tracking down Jessica and Elizabeth, sneaking up on them in the deserted woods, and thrusting forward with that long, gleaming knife—

The twins' father pounded his fist against his forehead. *I've got to find my daughters before Marin gets to them,* he thought. *I've just got to.*

The sky was deepening to a dark, purplish blue. The ocean mirrored its color, with white strips of foam gleaming along the crests of waves. A flash of silent lightning streaked the horizon. Elizabeth realized that a storm was brewing. She was surprised not to have noticed it before.

If she hadn't felt so nervous and alone, Elizabeth would have liked to write a poem about the dramatic view of dusk from the narrow path she and Fred the Horse were negotiating. She could barely make out Jessica in front of her, on Black Beauty, whose nervous hooves sent occasional showers of rock skittering over the cliff.

Suddenly another pattering of falling rocks made Elizabeth whirl in her saddle. The noise had come from behind her. *That's stupid,* she scolded herself in a low voice. *The only other person around is Jessica, and she's in front of me. I must've heard an echo.*

She shivered. Elizabeth's short-sleeved T-shirt and walking shorts did almost nothing to ward off the worsening chill in the air. And as much as she tried to push the thoughts away, the sight of the wind-tossed Pacific Ocean at night brought back a rush of memories of being in danger and full of fear on the deck of Marin's sailboat.

Elizabeth nudged Fred into a slightly faster walk, to catch up with Jessica and Black Beauty. But the path was too dangerous to allow the horses to move with any real speed. And the quickly falling darkness didn't help.

A lumpy, vertical shape seemed to jump suddenly from a pile of rocks. Elizabeth gasped. She reined her horse so quickly that he almost sat down on his hind legs.

"Liz!" Jessica's voice came back down the path to her. "What's wrong?" Her twin appeared suddenly out of the gloom.

Elizabeth tried to catch her breath. "It's nothing," she assured her. "One of those funny tall cactus plants startled me, that's all."

"I know what you mean," Jessica said. "I keep having the same problem." She began describing her own encounters with plant life. She spoke bravely, but to Elizabeth her voice sounded more subdued than usual—as if she were afraid that speaking too loudly would awaken whatever unknown terrors were hidden in the darkness.

Elizabeth shook her head. She had to stop thinking like a character in an Edgar Allan Poe poem. Instead she latched on to her sister's voice and urged Fred to follow it, grateful for its utter normality.

Suddenly she heard a clattering sound, coming from close behind her. *"Who's there?"* Elizabeth called.

"What's wrong?" Jessica asked nervously.

"I don't know," Elizabeth whispered. "I could've sworn I heard something behind us—like another horse."

"It's that writer's brain of yours, working overtime," Jessica said bravely. "I bet it was just an echo."

"I'm sure that's it," Elizabeth said, hoping it was true. "Our voices must be bouncing off these cliffs."

"Or maybe it was a seagull," Jessica suggested.

Elizabeth nodded. "Maybe." A clatter in front of her interrupted her thoughts. "Jessica? Are you all right?" Her sister didn't answer immediately. "Jessica!"

"It's OK, Liz," Jessica called, sounding out of breath. "The trail is narrower and rockier here. Black Beauty stumbled. Don't look off the edge to your left. It'll make you dizzy."

Elizabeth nodded and turned Fred's head to the other side. He had no objections to keeping as close as possible to the rock wall that rose to their right. "Mom and Dad must be worried sick about us," Elizabeth said. "The horseback ride was supposed to be over by six o'clock. That was two hours ago."

She whirled in her saddle again, sure she had heard a noise off to one side. But she could make out only the dim shapes of lurking rocks behind her.

"So much for getting Dad to chill out about us being safe," Jessica said. "Once we get back to the hotel tonight, he won't let us out of his sight for the rest of the week."

"I just hope we *reach* the hotel tonight," Elizabeth replied. "If we do, I don't care if Dad watches us all week like Chrome Dome Cooper himself!"

Jessica giggled nervously at the mention of Sweet Valley High's hawk-eyed principal. Then Elizabeth heard another clatter from up ahead.

"Be real careful here, Liz," Jessica warned a moment later in a breathless voice. She had just rounded a bend and was no longer visible from Elizabeth's position. "There's been a rock slide, I guess, and the path turns in really sharply. Black Beauty almost stepped over the edge."

"Are you OK?" Elizabeth asked quickly, alarmed.

"I'm OK, Liz," Jessica called back to assure her in a shaky voice. "So's Black Beauty. It's just that—" Her voice was cut short in a rattle of rock fall.

"Jessica!" Elizabeth spurred her horse closer. She gasped as she rounded the bend.

Black Beauty had dropped to one knee on the very edge of the precipice. Now the mare struggled to regain her footing, whinnying in terror at the sharp drop-off just below her nose. Jessica lay on the horse's back, flung forward against her neck, clinging frantically to the black mane. The saddle had come loose and was hanging uselessly around the mare's heaving flanks. The girl and the horse were silhouetted against a sky full of swirling purple clouds.

"Don't come any closer!" Jessica ordered in a tense whisper.

Elizabeth reined Fred in tightly. If Jessica or the mare made a single wrong move, both would go plummeting over the cliff.

"Well, well, well," said a mocking voice behind her. The voice sent terrible shivers up Elizabeth's spine. For a horrible moment she thought she was going to faint. She slowly turned around to see

Brad's huge reddish horse carefully making its way around the bend. But on its back sat John Marin, his perfect teeth flashing like stars through the murky evening.

"Marin!" Elizabeth whispered.

Jessica screamed, and the black mare pitched forward.

"Jessica!" yelled Elizabeth.

Chapter 8

Elizabeth froze. On the edge of the cliff, Black Beauty neighed helplessly. Jessica clung desperately to the horse's back.

As Elizabeth held her breath, the mare scrambled and managed to check her slide down the slope, but Jessica and Black Beauty were still in grave danger. The horse's mouth foamed like the waves that crashed against the sharp rocks eighty feet below. And every time the mare tried to stand up, the rocks under her shod feet slid her farther forward, over the cliff. Jessica's slightest movement threw her even more off balance. And John Marin watched the scene with a calm, amused expression on his face.

"Run, Liz!" Jessica yelled. "Don't wait for me!"

Elizabeth nudged Fred closer to the fallen mare. "Slide backward down the horse's back, Jess,

135

and then jump off!" Elizabeth urged her sister. She stopped and looked over her shoulder. Marin, on Big Red, was swaying toward them. "You can do it, Jessica!" Elizabeth cried. "Hurry!"

Marin reined his horse in the middle of the path and sat grinning at them, two horse lengths away. "You've got yourself in quite a pickle, Jessica," he called. "Some girls just don't know how to stay out of trouble."

"Ignore him, Jessica," Elizabeth commanded. "Do as I said. Slide back slowly—don't scare the horse!"

"I can't, Liz," Jessica called. "The slope's too unstable. I'll fall! You go. Get away from Marin now! You've still got a chance."

Marin laughed but made no move to come closer. "Isn't this a touching scene?"

Elizabeth's mind raced. *Jessica can make it,* she thought, *if she takes her time and doesn't panic. I have to keep Marin away from her. It's her only chance.* She caught her sister's eye for a moment and saw Jessica's almost imperceptible nod.

Elizabeth turned to the grinning horseman, subtly maneuvering the frightened Fred as she spoke, so that he stood between Big Red and Black Beauty. "What's your problem, Marin?" she asked in her toughest voice. "A little identity crisis, maybe? Are you having trouble deciding who to be today?"

"An intriguing opening, Elizabeth," Marin said

136

with a chuckle. "It sounds like the kind of metaphysical ranting you and Ben Morgan were so fond of."

At the mention of Marin's alias—the one Elizabeth had fallen for—she clenched her teeth, determined not to lose her temper or her nerve. "If you were Ben right now, you'd be rushing forward to help us," she told him. "If you were John Marin the maniac, you'd probably be spooking Jessica's horse to send them both over the edge. Who are you now? It's not like you to sit back and watch."

Marin laughed. "It's a shame to kill two girls as amusing as you two. Why should I be doing anything besides sitting back to watch? You'll both die soon enough, whether it's from plummeting over the cliff or bleeding to death when I stab your warm, supple bodies." He wiped his mouth with the back of his hand. "Why shouldn't I get some entertainment first?"

Good job, Liz, Jessica thought. *Keep Marin talking. Keep him distracted while I find a way out of this.*

Her twin had been right—Jessica could slide off the horse to safety—but only if Black Beauty stayed still and didn't panic. How in the world could Jessica keep the skittish mare calm? Black Beauty couldn't regain her footing on the broken rocks; for all Jessica knew, the mare might actually be injured. Even if she wasn't injured, it would be nearly impossible for the horse to rise to her feet and move away from the edge—while carrying Jessica on her back. And one slip could send them both over the cliff.

The sight of the churning ocean below made Jessica's stomach churn, too. She turned her head. *This is just like climbing a rope in gym class,* she told herself. *If you get scared, you keep your eyes glued to the rope. Don't look down, no matter what happens.*

That's it! Jessica realized. She had to keep Black Beauty from looking down. She remembered hearing about a farmer who threw gunnysacks over horses' heads to keep them calm as they were led from a burning barn. It was worth a try. She had to cover Black Beauty's eyes so that the horse wouldn't panic until they were both away from the ledge.

"Where's a gunnysack when you need one?" Jessica muttered under her breath.

"How did you find us here?" Elizabeth asked Marin.

Good going, Liz, Jessica thought. *Keep stalling him. I just need a little more time.*

"Why, darling, you know I'd follow you and your sister to the ends of the earth," Marin replied. "I promised your daddy I'd be back for you. And I never forget a promise."

Jessica stopped listening. She frantically untied

the blue cotton sweater from around her waist. Then she threw it over the horse's bucking head. A shudder ran through the mare's body, jarring Jessica's already jangled nerves. Then Black Beauty quieted, as if by magic. Jessica began to slide slowly backward down the horse's broad, long back. Just a few inches more, and she'd be able to jump to stable ground.

"And then that redheaded waitress told me you'd gone horseback riding," Marin said, his smug voice penetrating Jessica's frantic thoughts. She realized that Marin was almost finished telling Elizabeth how he'd tracked down the twins. Her time was running out.

Suddenly a flash of lightning seared across the sky, followed by a boom of thunder that echoed against the cliffs. Black Beauty tossed her huge head, terrified. The cotton sweater dropped away and disappeared over the edge of the cliff. The horse screamed, a loud, terrifying sound like nothing Jessica had ever heard before.

She leaped backward off Black Beauty's heaving sides and landed near Elizabeth and Fred. Marin's mouth formed a grim line, and his eyes shone in the strange purplish-green glow of the sky at twilight before a storm.

"Jessica! Jump!" Elizabeth screamed, reaching a hand down as Fred began to bound away from Marin.

The twins' great-great-grandmother, Jessamyn,

had been a bareback rider in the circus. Jessica felt her ancestor's blood coursing through her own veins as she leaped toward her sister's hand. In an eye blink she was astride Fred, behind Elizabeth. She entwined her arms around her sister and helped kick the horse into a gallop along the rocky, narrow trail. "Giddyap, Fred!" Jessica yelled.

From the corner of her eye, she saw Black Beauty, now unburdened, struggling to her feet. But the image vanished as Fred picked up speed.

Behind Jessica, hooves pounded on the hard path as the first spatters of rain began to hit her face. Marin was chasing them. And he obviously had the faster horse.

Mrs. Wakefield held up a red tube of fabric, puzzled as to what its purpose might be. Then she realized it was a dress, and she grinned wryly. Like everything else she'd found in Elizabeth and Jessica's hotel room, the dress left no question as to which twin owned it.

She folded the skimpy dress into Jessica's light-blue suitcase. It was the last personal belonging to be packed. She shook her head at the thought of her own daughter wearing such a thing. But she never would have dreamed of forbidding her. In eighteen years of motherhood, Mrs. Wakefield had learned to choose her battles. It was all a matter of perspective. Some parents flew off the handle over clothes and haircuts. But such trappings were trivial. Other issues concerning her daughters were much more important. Some meant life or death.

Death, Mrs. Wakefield thought numbly. Only a week earlier John Marin had tried to kill her girls. *And now he might be trying again, at this very moment.*

She blinked back tears. She had to stay in control; she'd be no good to anyone if she fell to pieces. The Catalina police had already taken her statement about Marin. Now the police were out searching for the girls. So was her husband. Even the hotel stable had sent out some riders. But the police had instructed Mrs. Wakefield to stay behind, near the telephone. Everyone else was trying to save her daughters' lives, while all she could do was sit in a luxury hotel and wait. Her only contribution was to pack her family's bags for a hurried trip off the island. She felt utterly helpless.

Mrs. Wakefield realized with a start that she was pacing. She stopped herself, sat on the bed, and checked her watch. It was almost eight thirty. Her husband had been gone for three hours. She had heard nothing from him or the girls. A new fear gripped her heart. John Marin hated her husband with all his sick, twisted heart. What if Marin found Mr. Wakefield before Mr. Wakefield found the twins?

I don't care what the police said, she thought grimly. *I'm not waiting here all night, not knowing what's happening. I'll give them another*

141

hour. If I don't hear anything by then, I'm join-
ing the search.

The horse's hooves pounded beneath her, jarring Elizabeth's entire body. She wasn't sure how
long they had been galloping along the narrow
ledge. Jessica's mad leap onto Fred's back seemed
long ago. Elizabeth felt as if she had done nothing
all her life but bounce up and down in a saddle as
purple clouds and rocky outcrops tilted by. Straight
ahead, the half-moon was a pale, silvery lavender
behind a layer of clouds. It gave little light.
Elizabeth hoped Fred could see the treacherous
path better than she could.

To her left, she sensed rather than saw a void
where the path dropped off sharply above the
pounding surf. The path had been sloping downward for some time; surely they were much closer
to the beach than they'd been on the eighty-foot
headland. Still, they had a long way to go before
they reached solid ground. Until then a single
stumble or misstep would send Fred over the
edge, with Jessica and Elizabeth on his back.

"Good boy, Fred!" she encouraged the horse,
patting his cold, sweaty neck. "Keep it up!" She
bent low over him to reduce the wind resistance.
Behind her, she felt Jessica doing the same.

Suddenly, chilly particles began stinging her
face and arms; it took Elizabeth a minute to understand that it was raining. Her heart sank. Very soon

Fred would find the footing even more precarious.

"Faster, Liz!" Jessica screamed. Elizabeth could feel her sister's breath against her ear, but she could barely make out the words above the chilling wind. "I can see Marin behind us, Liz. He's getting closer!"

Elizabeth hated to cause pain to any animal, but she had no choice. She dug the heels of her sneakers into Fred's sides, and he responded with a short burst of speed.

"We can't get away!" Elizabeth called back to Jessica. "Fred can't keep this up much longer. He's too tired!"

"He has to!" Jessica shouted.

"I know," Elizabeth said. "But the path is awful, and Marin's horse is faster. We'll never make it!"

Jessica shifted on the horse. "We have to do something!"

Elizabeth saw a dark flash of movement from the corner of her eye. Marin's horse was coming up alongside Fred. *It's over,* she realized. The path was narrower just ahead. If she didn't rein in her horse, Marin would force them off the side of the cliff.

Elizabeth took a deep breath, preparing to give up and pull to a halt.

"Liz!" Jessica screamed, terrified. Her arms tightened around her sister's waist. Elizabeth could hardly breathe. She turned to see Marin reaching out for Jessica, trying to pull her off the horse.

"You can't get away from me!" he called with a burst of smug laughter.

The sound of his mocking laughter caused something to snap inside Elizabeth. Her fear was replaced by a burning, steaming rage. She refused to let Marin beat them. She wondered how high the cliff was at this point; then she realized that it didn't matter. Eight feet or eighty was all the same. Either way, she was going to do it. The crashing of the sea sounded louder than before, but the roaring in her ears and the howling wind made it impossible to tell how far below the waves might be. Lightning slashed across the sky, and the drizzle of rain grew to a real downpour.

"Hang on, Jessica!" she called, spurring the horse farther. "We're going over the side!"

At the edge of the rocky cliff, Elizabeth hesitated for only an instant. Then she jumped the horse out into the dark emptiness, feeling as if she were flying against the storm-ravaged sky and the silvery moon.

Mr. Wakefield reluctantly slowed his horse to a trot. Raindrops were splattering down through the trees, and the riding trail had become muddy and hard to follow. He hated to lose time, but he couldn't risk a fall. If Satchmo got injured, Mr. Wakefield would be stuck alone in the woods, with no way of reaching his daughters.

"Jessica!" he called into the darkened forest. "Elizabeth!"

"Hello!" called a voice from up ahead.

For one joyful instant Mr. Wakefield's heart leaped to his throat. Immediately his relief dissipated. The voice belonged to a man. Then three horses appeared on the trail in front of him. Two men in yellow rain slickers rode the first two. A large black mare was tied behind them and appeared to be limping. The black mare had no rider.

"Who are you?" one of the men demanded, shining a flashlight in Mr. Wakefield's face.

"Mr. Wakefield!" the other man called, holding up a lantern. He pulled off his glasses to wipe raindrops from the lenses. The twins' father recognized him as the stable hand who had rented Satchmo to him. "It's me, Joe!" he said. "And this is Brad, the trail guide who was leading your daughters' trip this afternoon."

"Is there any news of my girls?" Mr. Wakefield choked out.

Joe and Brad exchanged a glance that filled the twins' father with dread. Then Joe stared at him for a long, agonizing moment. In the glow of the lantern, Mr. Wakefield could see that the young man's eyes were full of pain.

"Nothing definite," Joe said, shaking his head. "But we found Jessica's horse." He gestured toward the limping mare.

Mr. Wakefield took a deep breath. "Where? What happened?"

"We found Black Beauty on the edge of a cliff overlooking the beach," Brad said. "Her knee is scratched up, but she's not hurt badly."

"So where's Jessica?" Mr. Wakefield asked. He couldn't stop his hands from trembling.

"We don't know," Joe said, his voice apologetic. "We found what looked like tracks from both girls' horses, leading out to the headland. At the edge of the cliff, the ground was scuffed up, as if a horse had lost its footing there."

"Our guess is that Black Beauty stumbled at the rim of the cliff," Brad said bluntly. "Jessica probably pitched right over the mare's head."

Mr. Wakefield felt his body go numb. "How high is that cliff?" he said, his voice almost a whisper.

Joe couldn't meet his gaze. "About eighty feet."

"Oh, no!" Mr. Wakefield gasped, a terrible shiver running through his whole body. He shook his head, refusing to believe the news.

"Sir, we really don't know for sure what happened," Joe said quickly. "We looked over the edge, but we couldn't see her at the bottom of the cliff. Maybe she never fell at all. Maybe she wasn't even on the horse when it stumbled."

Mr. Wakefield nodded, hoping the raindrops on his face would hide his tears. "Or maybe it was too dark for you to see her down there," he said. He gulped, struggling to keep his grief and horror under control. "What about Elizabeth?"

Brad shook his head. "There's no telling," he said. "We saw hoofprints from Liz's horse leading toward the ledge, but not coming back."

"Of course, that doesn't mean anything," Joe added. "The ground around there is mostly rock. She could have walked the horse away from the cliff without leaving a trace."

"We should all be getting back to the stable, Mr. Wakefield," Brad said. "Black Beauty's leg will need tending to, and we'll have to show the police what we found—"

His words were cut short by a warning look from Joe. Mr. Wakefield searched both men's faces. "What is it?" he asked. "What are you hiding from me?"

Joe sighed. "This," he said, pulling up a piece of bluish fabric from his saddlebag. "I'm sorry, Mr. Wakefield. I didn't want to worry you any further, since we're not completely sure of the situation."

The twins' father stared at what seemed to be a scrap torn from a cotton sweater. He forced himself to breathe. "What do you *think* it is?" he asked finally, taking the scrap from Joe.

Brad shrugged. "It looks a lot like a piece of the sweater Jessica had tied around her waist."

Mr. Wakefield felt as if he had been punched in the stomach. "Where did you find it?" he asked, dreading the answer.

Joe's eyes locked on to his face. "It was caught on a sharp rock, a few feet down the side of the cliff," he said in a shaky voice. "It was just below the place where Black Beauty stumbled."

The twins' father felt dizzy. He grabbed his saddle horn to keep from falling off the gelding.

"I'm afraid it gets worse," Brad said after a moment. "We found the tracks of a third horse, also heading out toward the edge of that cliff. I believe it was the horse that John Marin was riding."

Mr. Wakefield fought back panic. He closed his eyes tightly and took a deep breath, but he still almost felt like fainting.

"I am so sorry for all of this, sir," Joe repeated, his voice full of pain. "It's all my fault. If I hadn't gone against policy and rented that maniac a horse—"

The twins' father shook his head. "It's nobody's fault but John Marin's," he choked out. A moment later he added in a low whisper, "And my own."

Brad's voice was overly hearty. "I think the best thing for all of us right now is to get back to the stables," he said. "We'll get something hot to drink and wait for word from the police. Who knows? Maybe they've already found your daughters, safe and sound—"

"No!" Mr. Wakefield interrupted. "I'm not going back until I know for sure. I want to see the place where Jessica might have gone over the edge."

"You won't find anything on that cliff," Brad objected. "We already checked the area. And by now the rain will have turned the prints into mud puddles."

"I'm going to the bottom of the cliff," Mr. Wakefield insisted. "If Jessica fell, she may be on the beach injured."

"As the crow flies, that strip of beach is just through the woods, that way," Joe told him, pointing. "But you'll never make it on horseback. There used to be a trail that leads along the rim of the cliffs, but it's impassable now."

"There has to be a way," Mr. Wakefield said, his voice grim.

"The only way to scale the cliffs is by leaving your horse behind and rappelling down the side," Brad said. "And even an experienced climber couldn't do it in this rain."

"Why don't you let us take you back to the stable?" Joe offered. "The police—"

"Forget the police!" Mr. Wakefield cried. "I have to see for myself! What if Jessica is down there, hurt? It could take hours to get help to her if we have to run back for the authorities first."

"All right," Joe agreed. "There's a road to the north of here that leads from the hotel to a campground that's just off the beach. Look, why don't I come with you? I know the way—"

"I think you two have done enough," the girls' father said darkly. He closed his eyes for a moment, trying to calm himself. "You two go back for the police," he said in a voice that dared them to object. "Just tell me which way to go."

Joe nodded slowly. "Take the road to the coastline and then ride south along the beach. You can't miss the headland where we found Jessica's horse; it's the highest cliff overlooking the coast."

Without another word, Ned turned away from the other men and urged his horse northward, through the dripping trees. He had to know the truth, no matter how painful it might be.

As Fred leaped from the cliff, Jessica felt queasy—as if she were riding a roller coaster in a horror movie. She forced her eyes open and hung on to Elizabeth's waist. The night was gloomy. But far beneath the horse's body, the sandy beach glowed in the eerie light that reflected off the water.

The water, Jessica thought, focusing on the violent surf. The twins and the brave little horse were going to die. They were about to plunge into the ocean.

The ground tilted crazily below her, and a rocky ledge rushed toward the little horse. This was it. They would never even reach the water. They would crash into the granite ledge and die right there, on the rocks.

The pounding of ocean waves grew louder, until it filled Jessica's head. She heard herself screaming.

Then Fred's hooves met stone and the impact

slammed through Jessica's body. For an instant she felt as if all her bones were being crushed together. Then the horse bounded into the air.

Jessica realized, amazed, that she was alive. It didn't seem possible, but Fred was still flying down the side of the bluff, in a series of running leaps. Jessica closed her eyes and tried not to throw up.

Finally the motion stopped. Fred stood quietly on the beach, his sides slick with rain and sweat. And Jessica sensed solid ground beneath his hooves. She could hardly catch her breath. "We're alive!" she marveled, opening her eyes. She was still holding tightly to her sister's waist; she could feel Elizabeth panting.

Jessica stared in horror at the thirty-foot bluff that towered overhead. "I can't believe we jumped from up there."

Elizabeth shook her head, but it was a moment before she could speak. "We didn't do anything," she corrected her. "It was all Fred."

"Man, was it ever!" Jessica patted the horse's quivering flank. "Look at that cliff he came down. I'd have bet anything that it couldn't be done."

The bluff wasn't nearly as steep as the eighty-foot one that Black Beauty had nearly stumbled over. The higher cliff was now hidden around a bend. But the cliff they'd jumped from was clearly visible. It wasn't one sheer, vertical drop, as it had seemed from midair, but a series of steep walls and flat ledges—like a huge staircase with impossibly high steps. Fred had made the descent in a series of graceful bounds.

"What do they call that horse with wings?" Jessica asked. "The one from the mythology unit in English class? That's our Fred!"

"Pegasus," Elizabeth answered in a tense, faraway voice. Jessica followed her gaze and gasped.

The top of the bluff was black against the purplish sky. On its crest, in silhouette, a man sat on a large, powerful horse. His hair and the horse's mane streamed out in the wind like flags. Except for that, John Marin was perfectly still. But he stared down at the twins with a malevolence that was tangible, even from thirty feet below.

"Let's get out of here," Jessica whispered into her sister's ear, as if she were afraid Marin would overhear. "You said there was a campground up the beach, with a road that leads to the hotel. Which way is it?"

Wordlessly, Elizabeth turned the horse's head to the north, and they cantered along the beach. To their left, waves crashed against rocky outcroppings, inky black in the night. The salt spray spattered Jessica's bare arms and legs, slightly warmer than the fat, slimy raindrops that raised goose bumps on her skin.

For now she and Elizabeth were safe. But Marin would surely follow them. And he wouldn't give up until he had accomplished what he'd set out to do.

Chapter 9

Despite the rain, Satchmo kept up a brisk canter along the paved road. Mr. Wakefield's clothes stuck to him, cold and sopping wet. But his mind wasn't on the discomfort of riding in the storm. He had to get to the beach. He had to see for himself the place where Jessica might have fallen.

It was after nine o'clock, and the twins' father was making good time along the paved road. The campground and the beach should be no more than a half mile in front of him.

Suddenly he heard hoofbeats ahead on the dark road. A single horse was cantering in his direction. Was it Marin? He pulled Satchmo to a halt, drew him to the shadows at the edge of the road, and waited. A short, sturdy horse emerged from the gloom, its pace slow but determined. Mr. Wakefield squinted into the darkness. The horse had not one, but two riders. And their identical heads shone gold in the night, though both were soaked from the storm.

"Jessica! Elizabeth!" he cried as they passed.

At Elizabeth's sudden pull on the reins, the reddish horse spun so quickly that both twins nearly fell off. Elizabeth found her voice first. "Dad!" she cried. She directed the small, sturdy horse over to her father's side.

"Oh, Dad, you wouldn't believe who we saw!" Jessica cried, near hysteria. "John Marin is on the island!"

"I know, honey. I know," the twins' father said, reaching out to squeeze her shoulder. "I thought you were . . ." He broke off as he realized that he was crying, his tears mingling with the raindrops on his face. He swallowed, hard. "Are you both all right?"

Elizabeth nodded. "We're fine, Dad," she said, sounding close to exhaustion. "Just tired and wet."

"Me, too," he replied with a nod. "Come back to the hotel now. Your mother's waiting for us."

"What are we going to do?" Elizabeth asked.

"We're getting off the island tonight," Mr. Wakefield said.

"What about Marin?" Jessica's voice was barely audible over the wind and rain.

"The police are combing the interior for him now," her father said, trying to sound confident. "I'm sure they'll find him by daybreak." He said a

154

silent prayer of thanksgiving as Elizabeth's horse fell into step beside his.

The wind nearly tore the umbrella out of Mrs. Wakefield's hand as she hurried down the path to the stables. Not that it made much difference. The rain was blowing onto her from all sides. The twins' mother wasn't paying much attention to the weather, even though her white blouse and khaki slacks were decidedly damp. It was close to ten o'clock, and she hadn't yet heard a single word about her daughters' whereabouts.

She had to know where the twins were. She had tried to follow the police's instructions to remain near the phone. But by nine thirty she couldn't stand waiting anymore; she had to act. Mrs. Wakefield had asked the front desk to take any calls and to notify the authorities if new information came in. Then she'd headed for the stables.

"I'm Alice Wakefield," she told the young stable hand who was shaking out a yellow rain slicker inside the warm, dry stable. His glasses were foggy. Obviously, the man had just returned from being out in the storm, probably as part of a search party. "Are you Joe? Do you have any word of my daughters or husband? Did you find anything in the woods?"

The young man looked down, as if he couldn't bear to meet her eyes.

"What is it?" Mrs. Wakefield begged Joe. "Tell me, please!"

"We're . . . we're just not sure," the man stammered. "It might not mean anything at all."

Mrs. Wakefield's mouth went dry. "What?"

"I just got back and alerted the police," he said. "I tried to call you, but the front desk said you were joining the search."

"Tried to call me about what?" she asked.

"Please take off your raincoat and have a seat, ma'am," Joe said kindly. "The trail guide, Brad, is in the office, putting water on the stove for tea."

Mrs. Wakefield's voice dropped to a near whisper, but her words were desperate and hard-edged. *Would you please tell me what's going on? What did you find?*"

"We found Jessica's horse," Joe replied, "injured, but not badly." He gestured toward a nearby stall, where a glossy black mare ate hungrily from a leather pouch. "Her knee is scraped up, as if she fell on it."

"I don't understand what that means!" Mrs. Wakefield cried. "Where did you find the horse? Where are my daughters?"

"The mare was on an eighty-foot cliff, overlooking the ocean. From the marks in the dirt, I'd say she stumbled on the very edge." He shut his eyes for a moment. "If that's what . . . happened," he continued, haltingly, "the rider could have been pitched over Beauty's head—and over the cliff."

The twins' mother sat down hard on a wooden folding chair. "You don't mean . . ." Her voice trailed off.

Joe knelt in front of her and took her hand in his. "I'm not sure what I mean, ma'am. There are probably a dozen other explanations." He paused to wipe his eyes with the back of his hand. "I am so sorry about all of this. I never should have let that man rent a horse. . . ."

"I can't just sit here!" Alice cried. "I have to *do* something!"

"Your husband and the police are searching now to learn what really happened," Joe said. He hesitated. "But Jessica's sweater—"

"Jessica's sweater? You found my daughter's sweater?" Tears started streaming down Mrs. Wakefield's face. "Does that mean . . ." She couldn't finish the thought.

Joe ducked his head. "We're not sure it means anything yet. We found a piece of fabric caught on a spear of rock, just over the edge of the cliff. It may have been torn from the blue sweater your daughter had with her."

Mrs. Wakefield buried her face in her hands. "What about Elizabeth?" she whispered.

"We've found no sign of her or her horse."

The twins' mother glanced up at Joe, her eyes suddenly fierce and protective. "And Marin?" she asked.

Joe gulped. "We found tracks from three horses

near the site where Black Beauty stumbled. Two were traveling together—we assume they're Jessica's and Elizabeth's. The other horse was coming from a different direction. It may have been the one Marin was riding; the tracks were about the right size." He sighed deeply. "I'm sorry, Mrs. Wakefield. This is all my fault."

She rose to her feet, full of determination. "Do you know where the place is—where you found Jessica's horse? Could you direct me there?"

"Well, sure I could," said the stable hand. "But that wouldn't make much sense, ma'am. I mean, it's pouring outside, and it's black as pitch. The trails will be slippery and dangerous. Why don't we have some tea? I'll wait with you until the police or your husband returns with news. If they come back with nothing, I'll lead the next search party myself—and I'll stay out there until I find your girls."

"I don't want to have some tea!" Mrs. Wakefield insisted. "I'm taking a horse, and I'm going to look for my daughters—now!"

"Mrs. Wakefield, I don't think that would be a good idea. The police should be back soon. If you just wait—"

"I've waited long enough! I'm going to look for my girls," Mrs. Wakefield repeated obstinately. "If they're out in those woods, I intend to—"

She stopped, certain that she'd heard a sound outside.

Joe rose to his feet. "That must be the police," he said. "Maybe they have more information."

The wooden door swung open, and Mrs. Wakefield felt giddy with a sudden release of tension. Her husband stood in the doorway, soaking wet, with an arm around each of the twins. Their hair was plastered to their faces, and they were pale and shivering. But they were alive. Water streamed from their clothing and hair, forming a shining pool on the wooden floor.

"Mom!" Elizabeth cried, throwing herself into her mother's arms. A minute later the Wakefields were engulfed in a four-way hug. Mrs. Wakefield never wanted to let go of her daughters again.

"Our two horses are outside," her husband said to Joe and Brad, who had just joined them from the other room. "Fred there deserves an extra ration of oats tonight."

"Oh, really?" Brad asked.

"Fred saved our lives," Elizabeth said, admiration glowing in her eyes. "He was the real hero tonight."

"He's Pegasus!" Jessica piped in.

"He'll get extra oats, and a special rubbing down," Joe promised her. Alice noticed that his glasses had fogged up again as soon as the stable door opened. "Brad, you'd better bring the horses in," Joe continued. "They're only getting wetter, standing in the rain."

Brad opened his mouth as if to complain, but a

glance from Joe changed his mind. He trudged out the door and returned a moment later, leading a large gray horse with white speckles.

"I'd better notify the police that you're all OK," Joe said to the Wakefields. "Would you rather wait for the authorities here, or in your rooms at the hotel?"

Mr. Wakefield shook his head. "We're not waiting anywhere. As far as we know, John Marin is still on this island, so we're getting off it. Now."

"I know you're pretty upset," Brad said as he led the horse into a stall. "But you really should wait for the police. They'll want to speak with your daughters about what happened tonight with that maniac."

"They can speak with the girls on the mainland," Mrs. Wakefield told him in a voice that left no room to argue. "We're leaving as soon as we can get to the pier."

Elizabeth grabbed her father's arm. "Dad, if we can leave, Marin can leave, too! What's to stop him from getting on a boat and following us?"

"The police have talked to every boat operator on the island," said her mother. "Everyone who could give Marin passage has seen his photograph and has instructions to call the authorities if he tries to get off the island."

Mr. Wakefield turned to Joe. "Do you know what time the next channel boat leaves for San Pedro?"

Joe shook his head. "I'm sorry, sir, but you're way too late. The last channel boat of the day left before sundown."

Mrs. Wakefield felt desperate. Every instinct in her body told her to put as much distance as possible between her family and John Marin. "Does that mean we're trapped on Catalina for the night?" she asked, her voice rising.

Jessica snapped her fingers. "Maybe not! I read in a brochure that a helicopter service takes people on and off the island!"

"That's no good," said Brad as he led a second horse, a small roan, into the stable. "Helicopters can't fly in a storm like this."

Elizabeth crossed the room to the reddish horse's stall and began tenderly petting its wet muzzle. *Obviously,* Mrs. Wakefield realized, *the small horse is Fred.*

"There has to be another way to get to the mainland," Mr. Wakefield said.

"What about a charter service?" the twins' mother asked. "Someone on the island must have a boat we can rent."

"Sure," Joe answered. "There are several companies in Avalon that run charter tours or rent boats. You'll find them near the pier where the channel boat comes in. But at this time of night—"

"Then that's where we're going," Mr. Wakefield said. "I don't want my daughters to be on this island with Marin for one second longer than they have to be."

Joe nodded, a resigned look on his face. "All right," he said, coming to a decision. "Look, folks, my fiancée's mother runs a houseboat-rental service. It's almost ten o'clock, and her place has been closed for hours. But I'm sure she'll let you have a boat if I vouch for you."

"How do we get there?" asked the twins' father.

"I can take you in one of the Orizaba's electric Jeeps. But what about your luggage?"

"It's packed and waiting in our rooms," Mrs. Wakefield told him. "Can you have the hotel send it over on the channel boat in the morning?"

"No problem," Joe said. "I'll bring it to the landing myself."

The twins' mother wondered briefly why the young man with the fogged-up glasses was being so cooperative. Then she remembered his apologies and knew that he was torn by guilt about having lent Marin a horse. Mrs. Wakefield wasn't sure if she blamed him or not. At the moment it wasn't worth worrying about. The only thing that mattered was getting off the island. Getting home.

Elizabeth sat stiffly in the stern of the houseboat, feeling every chug of the engine through the wooden bench. The rain had died down to a drizzle. But in the heavy wind her damp hair slapped against her shoulders like a sheet on a clothesline.

"This boat sounds like a popcorn popper," Jessica complained. "Are you sure the motor's working OK?"

"It's fine," her father assured her from the helm. "The engine's just a little cold. And Mrs. Clayton said there's a big canister of extra gasoline, in case we need it."

"It was nice of her to stock the boat with coffee for us," the twins' mother called from the galley. "I've got a pot brewing. It'll be warm in a few minutes."

"Great!" her husband replied in a hearty voice. "Something hot to drink will do us all good. I'm glad the storm's over, but the wind has whipped up some heavy-duty waves."

Elizabeth's parents and sister went on discussing the boat, the coffee, and the storm—anything but John Marin and the reason for their hasty flight from the island. But Elizabeth's mind was elsewhere. She turned on the bench, leaning her arms on the brass railing, and cupped her chin in her palms. The lights of Catalina were receding behind the houseboat, into the fog and the distance. She knew she was leaving Marin far behind, but she felt he was nearer than ever. Something about being on a boat again brought him rushing closer, like a gale-force wind.

In a way, it was as if she'd never left the deck of Marin's sailboat the preceding Saturday night—as if everything that had happened since then was

163

only a dream. Reality was wind buffeting her face, waves slapping against the hull, and the hollow sound of the deck beneath her feet. Even the last twinkles of landlocked lights behind the boat could have been the lights of Sweet Valley Marina the week before, mirrored in the ink-black water and the gleaming blade of Marin's knife.

She shook her head violently, as if to dispel the image. "No," she whispered, "that was last Saturday. Tonight isn't the same at all." She forced herself to focus on the differences. The wind was colder and stronger than last week, spitting hard drops of rain that felt gritty against her skin. And the chugging motor was louder—more intrusive— than the billowing white sails of Marin's yacht. Last week she'd been alone with Marin. Now she was safe, her parents and sister only a few feet away.

Still, she couldn't help feeling the same sense of heightened reality she'd felt on the deck of Marin's boat, as the coast guard's lights had cast grotesque shadows on the sail behind them while she and Marin had struggled for the knife. And she couldn't help feeling dread rising within her until she felt as if she were suffocating.

She whirled at the touch of a hand on her bare arm.

"Elizabeth!" her mother said, her blue eyes anxious. "Didn't you hear us calling you from inside?"

"No, I guess I didn't," Elizabeth said.

"The coffee's ready, honey." Mrs. Wakefield

peered down at her daughter with warm concern. "Why are you sitting out here in the rain?" she asked.

"It's not raining anymore," Elizabeth said, noticing for the first time that the gritty drizzle had stopped.

"No, I guess not. But the wind's cold, and getting stronger. I wish I had thought to borrow a couple of sweatshirts from those men at the stable. You and Jessica are dressed as if it's still eighty degrees out."

Elizabeth shrugged, trying to hide her shivering. Her mother's comment made her more aware than ever of her short-sleeved shirt and khaki shorts. Her teeth chattered.

"Come inside and get something hot to drink," her mother instructed. "Maybe we can find some blankets for you and your sister."

Elizabeth allowed herself to be led into the cabin. But she stopped in the doorway and turned for one last look at the coast of Catalina Island. She was too late. The lights of the shore had vanished behind a shroud of fog. Elizabeth felt terribly alone.

"I can't wait until tomorrow," the man insisted. "I need a boat now!"

"I'm sorry, mister," the gray-haired woman said. The porch light above showed a suspicious look on her face. "But we closed at five."

She tried to shut the door of the boat-rental office, but Marin shoved his broad shoulder into the doorway. He knew why the woman was at the office more than five hours after closing. He knew Ned Wakefield. And he was sure that the counselor would have got his family off the island as soon as he possibly could. Marin had no choice but to follow. It was the only way to make Wakefield pay for putting him behind bars—not once, but twice.

Besides, the Wakefields would certainly have alerted the authorities. The police were probably combing the island already, searching for Marin. He had to get away. He wasn't planning on ever going back to prison.

When Marin had seen the lights on inside the Clayton Boat Rentals office, he'd known exactly who had been by so late in the evening to rent a boat. Now it was Marin's turn to do the same—if the police or the coast guard hadn't already reached this woman with his description and photo. He tried to read her expression. Did she know who he was and why he wanted a boat? Or was she balking simply because of the hour?

"Even if it weren't after closing, I couldn't rent you a boat tonight," Mrs. Clayton told him. "I rented out my last houseboat this evening." She was obviously trying to keep her voice casual, but she couldn't hide the edge of suspicion in it. She glanced over her shoulder, and Marin caught sight of a flyer on the desk inside the office. He was too far away to read it.

"There's an old wooden motorboat tied up at the dock," Marin said quickly. "I'll take that one." *It's just as well,* he decided. The Wakefields must have rented that last houseboat. He would need something faster, like the sixteen-foot boat with its outboard motor, to catch them.

"That's *my* motorboat," Mrs. Clayton objected. "It's not a rental."

Marin wanted to smack the old biddy across the face. Instead he flashed her his most endearing smile. "I only need it for a few hours," he said.

"I don't care if you only need it for a few seconds," she retorted. "It's not for rent."

Marin pulled his wallet from the back pocket of his new jeans. "I'll pay you a hundred dollars."

The woman glanced around herself uncertainly, as if looking for guidance. "All right," she decided finally. "Wait here while I get the paperwork."

When she stepped into the room, Marin pretended to be inspecting the tethered boat bobbing on the waves. But from the corner of his eye, he watched her through the crack in the door. She lifted the sheet of paper from the desk, and her eyes flitted between the flyer and his face in the doorway. Realization dawned in her eyes, replaced quickly with fear.

Marin smiled. He threw open the door and crossed the room in two long strides. He swung his fist and felt a satisfying thud as it landed against the side of her head. The woman dropped like a rag doll.

Marin snatched the flyer off the floor where it had fallen. His own face stared back at him. He laughed and closed his fist around the paper, pretending it was Ned Wakefield's high-and-mighty neck. "That's what you get for sticking it out so often," he said with a chuckle. "That's what you get, Ned!"

On a hook near the door, Marin found the ignition key to the motorboat. He grabbed a pair of binoculars off a shelf. Then he broke the glass cover of the fire-extinguisher box and tore the ax from its rack. *You never know when an extra weapon might come in handy,* he thought, grinning to himself.

"Thank you, Mrs. Clayton," he said to the woman's prostrate form. "It's been a pleasure doing business with you."

As he climbed into the motorboat, Marin realized he still held the balled-up flyer in his hand. He tossed it into the sea and watched it bob on the surface for a moment, glowing ghostly white, until it disappeared into the water's blackness. Then he started the motor and steered the boat out of the dock.

Jessica poured herself a second cup of hot coffee and pulled the thin cotton blanket tighter around her shoulders. "How much longer until we get to the mainland?"

"I'm not sure how to estimate," her mother called from the ship's wheel just outside the open cabin door. "The channel boat takes only an hour or so. I'm afraid it could take a lot longer in this thing. It's dark, and the waves are rough. We have to take it slowly."

Mr. Wakefield looked up. He'd been staring at a navigation chart as if he were trying to convince his family that he really knew how to read it. Jessica knew that her parents were no strangers to boats, but they weren't experts, either. Elizabeth was a little more knowledgeable than the rest of the family, but not by much. "If this weren't an emergency," Mr. Wakefield admitted, "I'd say it's not really safe to be out here at all. But we didn't have any choice."

"No, we didn't," Elizabeth whispered. Her face was pale in the dim cabin, and she was shivering, despite the blanket wrapped around her. Jessica wondered if she was sick.

Jessica turned to the round window and looked outside. The moon had set, and the black sky was indistinguishable from the dark water. If not for the streaky reflections of their own lights in the waves close to the boat, Jessica could almost have believed they were traveling through space. Suddenly a white blur shone for an instant, then was swallowed up in a wave.

"What was that?" she asked.

Her father jumped up. "What was what?"

Jessica watched as the white blur rose on the crest of another wave and seemed to come into focus. "Dad, it's a motorboat."

"Marin!" Elizabeth whispered, kneeling beside her on the bunk to look out the same window.

Jessica saw her father's face turn white as he peered through the next window. "No!" he said in a tense voice. "It can't be him."

"Why can't it be?" Elizabeth asked.

"Marin couldn't be following us," her father said, his voice shaky. "He has no way of knowing we've left Catalina. Even if he did know, the police and the coast guard would never let him off the island. It's just not possible."

Jessica felt numb. "What if it is?" she asked. "What if he's coming for us . . ."

"No," her father repeated. He sounded more certain this time. "That can't be Marin. Look—that boat is in trouble. Marin's too methodical to get himself into a jam like that."

"What kind of trouble?" Mrs. Wakefield asked from the helm.

"It's being tossed around on the waves as if the motor's dead," Elizabeth said in a voice that sounded tense but no longer afraid.

Her father nodded. "Yes, it's foundering, all right. I want to get a better look."

Jessica tossed off her blanket and followed her

170

father out the cabin door. A blast of cold air enveloped her as she stepped out into the night. Behind her, she heard Elizabeth rise to join the rest of the family on the deck. Mr. Wakefield cupped his hand around his eyes to cut the glare from the houseboat's lights and stood at the railing.

"Can you tell what's happening?" Mrs. Wakefield asked. "Should I steer toward it?"

"No!" her husband said. "If the current's worse over there, we don't want to get sucked in, too."

At the wheel the girls' mother bit her lip. "Can you see anyone on the boat?"

"I can't tell," Jessica announced, leaning over the railing to peer into the gloom. "It's got one of those canvas covers pulled over the front half of it."

"Damn!" her father swore. "I wish I had thought to rent a pair of binoculars."

Elizabeth stifled a scream as a wave crashed over the smaller boat. "It's going to capsize!"

Jessica held her breath until the little white boat bobbed to the crest of another wave, streaming dark water.

"Ned, we have to do something," Mrs. Wakefield said.

"I know," her husband replied. "I'll take the inflatable dinghy and see if I can help."

"The dinghy? Ned, no! It's too dangerous in such a small boat, with the water so rough. Let's take the houseboat over to it."

171

"No! I'm going alone. In the meantime, see if you can raise the coast guard on the radio."

"Why don't I try that first?" his wife suggested. "You stay here, and we'll let the coast guard handle it."

"We can't, Mom," Elizabeth said, her face sad. "There's no time. Look at it. That boat won't last long out there, if its motor's down. Look how low it's riding. It must have taken on some water. There might be a hole in the hull."

Her mother nodded. "You're right. We have to try to help, if we can. Let's cast the anchor. Then you girls and I can help your father lower the dinghy into the water."

John Marin watched the progress of the mustard-colored dinghy through his binoculars. He sat inside the motorboat's canvas cover, peeking around its edge, so his body was hidden from the Wakefields. He was almost certain that they wouldn't be able to recognize him at this distance, but this was no time for unnecessary risks. It might be his last chance at Ned Wakefield and his sickeningly wholesome family. And there was always the chance that one of the Wakefields had a pair of binoculars, too.

Mr. Wakefield was heading toward the motorboat, alone in the little inflatable raft. He was rowing like crazy. The night was black, but Mr. Wakefield's yellowish boat and orange life preserver practically glowed in the dark, making him easy to spot. A pinprick of light shone momentarily, and Marin realized that the counselor was carrying a flashlight.

"Good try, Ned," Marin whispered to himself. "But you're too far away for that light to help you see what's really out here. And by the time you're close enough, it'll be too late."

Marin smiled to see that the tide was against the man. Waves crashed on the front of the little boat, spraying the counselor with sporadic showers of seawater.

"That's right, Counselor," Marin said. "I knew you couldn't stand by and let a stranger die. You heroic types are so predictable." He kicked at the water that was filling the bottom of the motorboat. It was seeping in through a small hole Marin had chopped in the hull using the fire-extinguisher ax. He laughed, watching the dinghy's progress and fingering the heavy ax blade.

As he'd been expecting, a sudden burst of static squawked from the radio in the front of the boat. Marin ducked under the canvas cover to answer Mrs. Wakefield's call for help.

"Mayday, Mayday!" came her sweet, urgent voice. "Does anybody read me?"

Marin picked up the transmitter. "This is coast guard station one-oh-nine, reading you loud and clear," he said, pitching his voice lower than usual. "What seems to be the problem?"

Mrs. Wakefield described the location of the foundering motorboat, and Marin assured her that he'd send help.

"There's just one more thing, ma'am," he added, suddenly inspired. "Because of the storm, a lot of emergency calls like yours are coming through, jamming the frequency. Now that we're aware of your situation, I'd appreciate it if you'd stay off the radio for the next hour or so—except, of course, in the case of another emergency."

The twins' mother agreed, and Marin hung up the transmitter and laughed. She was just as predictable as her husband. Then he swung the ax at the radio, and it ruptured in a shower of sparks.

Again he trained the binoculars on the houseboat. Jessica and Elizabeth stood on the deck, side by side. Against the black of the night, one twin's arms looked bone-white in the boat's deck lights. That was Jessica, Marin decided, taking note of her loose hair and bare midriff. Elizabeth's hair was pulled back; a blanket swaddled her shoulders. Still, they looked more alike than different. Two identical heads gleamed gold, and two identical hands shielded their eyes as the twins' gazes followed their father's progress.

"Don't worry, girls," Marin muttered. "First I'll take care of your precious father. Then it's your turn—you and your pretty little mother." He smiled. Wakefield's wife was standing on the deck of the houseboat, looking sexy, as always—even at this distance, and on a dark night.

"You can't escape from me this time, ladies," Marin said, running his thumb along the ax blade. "Ned Wakefield's worst nightmares are about to come true."

Marin scurried under the tarp to the front of the boat long enough to scrawl something on a sheet of paper. He attached it to the steering wheel on a clip that was meant for a map. Then he crawled back outside, into the wind, and squinted across the jagged waves at the spot of gold that he knew was Mr. Wakefield's life raft.

"Next time, Ned, don't believe everything you see," Marin told the figure approaching over the waves. "Of course, there won't be a next time for you—or your family."

He let the rush of salt-tangy wind wash over his body like a waterfall. He breathed deeply, feeling the power of the wind entering him, making him stronger. He checked to make sure the boat's ladder was hanging over the hull, like a welcome mat for an old friend. Then he slipped over the opposite side of the boat—still clutching the ax in his hand—and waited in the dark, cold water.

"Hello!" Mr. Wakefield called into the wind as he pulled the inflatable dinghy up alongside the motorboat. "Is anybody there?"

No one answered his hail. He shone his flashlight along the length of the boat, but the disk of yellow light seemed pathetic against the huge, storm-tossed darkness of the ocean at night. Something metal glinted in the weak beam of the flashlight. An aluminum ladder hung from the side of the boat.

That's strange, Mr. Wakefield thought. *Who'd leave out the ladder in a storm like this?* He began to swing his body onto the ladder, but the oversize life jacket impaired his movements. Impatiently, he yanked it over his head and tossed it back into the dinghy. Then he climbed the ladder and tied the dinghy's line to the motorboat. Water splashed around his feet as he landed on the deck.

Liz had been right, he saw. The motorboat was taking on water quickly. *There must be a hole in the hull,* he thought. *This thing won't be afloat for long.*

He poked his head under the canvas cover and peered into the darkness beneath, sweeping his flashlight in an arc. "Anybody here? I've got a boat tied up alongside. I can get you to safety," he called.

Mr. Wakefield's eyes adjusted to the darkness, and he realized that he was speaking to the empty night. Somehow the motorboat's occupants had left. He lowered himself into the driver's seat, perplexed. What had happened? Why was there nobody in the boat? Had someone fallen overboard?

Had the occupants been rescued? Maybe there had never been anyone there, he considered. Perhaps the boat had broken away from its moorings, empty, and been swept out to sea.

Then he noticed something white on the steering wheel. He shone his flashlight on a sheet of paper that was clipped to the wheel and read the hastily scrawled writing on it:

"You lose, Counselor. Alice and the girls are mine."

Bile rose in Mr. Wakefield's throat. Marin had been playing with him all along. The foundering motorboat was a setup. Marin was no doubt on the houseboat with his wife and daughters already—or on his way there.

Marin is with Alice and the twins, Mr. Wakefield's mind echoed in horror. Panic gripped him, and he rushed to the side of the boat where he'd left the dinghy. He was halfway down the ladder before he noticed that the inflatable craft was gone. He peered into the distance and caught a glimpse of brighter color on the black waves. His own orange life jacket bobbed along with the rubber boat. At this distance, and in the dark, the twins' father couldn't make out the features of the man in the life jacket. But he knew exactly who it was.

Marin. And the killer was well on his way toward the girls and their mother.

Still clutching the ladder, Mr. Wakefield peered

farther into the distance. He looked toward what would have been the horizon, if the night had been light enough to differentiate between sea and sky. And there he saw what he was looking for. The houseboat's hazy hull materialized in snatches, bouncing through the mist like a gull caught in an upwind. But something was different about the houseboat. He saw a pinpoint of dazzling yellow light, intense enough to cut through the fog. His wife must have turned it on to guide him back. Unfortunately, now it could only help Marin.

The twins' father climbed back up the ladder. *I have to find a way to save my family,* he thought desperately.

He swept the interior of the motorboat with his flashlight. A pair of binoculars lay on a seat, just inside the canvas boat cover. Without them all he could see of the houseboat was that yellow light and an occasional blur of hazy white—if he knew where to look. With the powerful binoculars, he could see his daughters on the deck, staring over the side as if trying to catch sight of his dinghy.

Mr. Wakefield examined the dark stretch of ocean between himself and the houseboat. His grip tightened on the cold, slick metal of the binoculars as he found the dinghy. A wave crashed over Marin's head as he rowed the little craft with muscular, sure strokes. Marin continued, his body pumping backward and forward, the fountain of water causing hardly a break in his strong, overhand stroke. He was gliding toward the houseboat at a steady pace, and the waves were helping to push him closer and closer.

For an instant the twins' father poised his body to dive from the motorboat and follow Marin through the water. But reason won out. Mr. Wakefield was in excellent shape for a man his age. But the waves were treacherous and the distance long. And Marin had an enormous head start. Heartsick, Mr. Wakefield realized that he didn't have a chance of overtaking the younger man before he reached the houseboat. In fact, he admitted, he had little chance of surviving at all in the rough, cold seas for more than a few minutes.

But he still had to find a way to help his family. If only he could somehow signal his wife to pull up anchor and outrun the dinghy. Then she could radio the coast guard to capture Marin and rescue her husband.

"A radio!" Mr. Wakefield yelled, sprinting to the front of the boat. Most boats that size didn't have a radio, but maybe this one did.

It did. But of course Marin had damaged it beyond repair, hacking it into a useless mass of burned-out circuits and crumpled bits of sharp metal.

"Dammit!" Mr. Wakefield swore. But his voice was lost in the howling of the wind, the thundering of the sea, and the ominous creaking of the slowly sinking boat. Suddenly one end of the canvas cover sprang loose in a gust of wind. It began to flap loudly against the edge of the windshield, sending splatters of cold water onto his already wet hair.

Impatiently, he tore off the cover and threw it onto the deck. What did it matter if he had a roof over his head? He was already soaking, and the canvas only blocked his view.

"But what good is seeing him if I can't stop him?" he demanded angrily. As he sank onto the front seat, he caught sight once again of the note still attached to the steering wheel. The bluish letters, once hard and angular, were now rounding out, becoming splotchy and growing spidery tendrils, as drops of water splattered them. But the words were still the same:

"You lose, Counselor. Alice and the girls are mine."

"No!" Mr. Wakefield screamed at the hazy gold dinghy that was still visible in the distance.

His foot disturbed something metallic on the floor. It was the ignition key for the boat. He shook his head. Marin was evil and warped, but he wasn't stupid. If the key was still on the boat, it was only because the boat wouldn't work. Or because Marin knew it would sink before Mr. Wakefield could take it anywhere.

The twins' father turned the key in the ignition and was greeted by the dull whine of a motor that refused to turn over. He pounded his fist against the dashboard. "Start, dammit! I have to keep Marin away from my family!"

But it seemed that the contest between the lawyer and the murderer was over, and that Ned Wakefield had lost. Twisted with hatred and vengeance, Marin was nearing the houseboat where Alice and the twins waited. Meanwhile, the girls' father was trapped on a sinking motorboat, with little hope for rescuing himself, let alone his family.

He had never felt so helpless.

Chapter 10

—

Jessica stepped into the houseboat's cabin, grateful to be out of the wind. Elizabeth had come inside from the deck a few minutes earlier and was seated on the edge of the double bunk. Jessica sat down next to her. She pulled the blue blanket that was wrapped around Elizabeth's shoulders around herself as well, so that it enveloped both twins.

Vaguely, Jessica remembered the oppressive heat of the forest in midafternoon, and the longing to feel the wind through her hair. The guided horseback ride seemed like ages ago; now Jessica felt as if she'd been cold and damp forever.

Elizabeth acted oblivious to Jessica's arrival. She sat on the bunk, staring at her fingers. Jessica noticed that her twin's nails had been chewed down to ragged squares. Elizabeth obviously needed some help relaxing. And Jessica knew just the right person for the job.

Jessica tweaked one of the blond tendrils that had sprung loose from her sister's ponytail. "At least our hair's finally dry!" she exclaimed in a flippant tone. "I guess mine must be as straggly looking as yours."

Elizabeth didn't look up. "Thanks a lot, Jess. It's great the way you always know exactly what to say to make a person feel better."

Jessica sighed. Elizabeth was in one of her sarcastic moods. But Elizabeth needed cheering up, and Jessica knew that nobody could do it better than she could. "As soon as all this is over," Jessica said cheerfully, "I'm going to take the world's longest, hottest shower and wash my hair. Then I'll pour about half a bottle of that mega-expensive new conditioner into it." She gave a playful tug on her sister's ponytail. "You want me to save the other half of the bottle for you?"

Elizabeth whirled. "How can you worry about your *hair* at a time like this?"

"I just—"

"Dad is out there in those terrible waves, on a flimsy little life raft!" Elizabeth interrupted. "Aren't you afraid for him?"

Jessica's good spirits vanished like mist in a strong wind. She scooted her body across the bunk, to lean against the wall.

Elizabeth sighed. "Jess," she said softly, "I'm

sorry. I didn't mean to snap at you." She slid over and rested her head against her sister's shoulder.

"Of course I'm afraid," Jessica admitted. "I thought I was trying to cheer you up. I guess I was trying to cheer myself up, too."

Elizabeth squeezed her hand. "Where's Mom?"

"She's pulling out the medical supplies from the storage compartment under the deck," Jessica said. "I asked if I could help, but she told me to come in and put on some more water for hot drinks."

Elizabeth's eyes widened. "Medical supplies? Does she think Dad's hurt?"

"No," Jessica replied, "but he might rescue some people from that motorboat. If he does, she thought they might need—I don't know, bandages or something."

"Oh, yeah. I guess so. You know, Dad's been gone so long I had almost forgotten about the people on the motorboat." Elizabeth closed her eyes. "Jessica, I'm worried about him."

"He hasn't been gone *that* long!" Jessica protested.

Elizabeth opened her eyes. "How would you know?" she asked.

"Don't get sarcastic again about that wristwatch thing," Jessica snapped. "Just because I never wear a watch does not mean I have no sense of time."

"Well, it sure doesn't mean—"

"All I'm saying is that it doesn't seem like it's been that long!" Jessica interrupted. "Remember,

Dad had to row the dinghy all the way to the motorboat, help the people he finds there, and make it all the way back here."

"Jess, it's eleven thirty," Elizabeth said sadly. "He's been gone three quarters of an hour."

"So?" Jessica countered. "The motorboat was far away, and you know what the waves are like."

"Yes, I do," her sister said. "That's what I'm afraid of."

"There's no reason to be afraid," Jessica assured her, trying to swallow her own fear. "Dad's good at rowing. Don't you have to steer the raft kind of back and forth in diagonal lines when the waves are against you?"

"Something like that," Elizabeth said. "It's called tacking."

"Well, that would take a long time," Jessica insisted. "And he's probably taking it slowly and carefully, just to be on the safe side."

"We should see him coming back toward us by now," Elizabeth said.

"I think it's foggier than it was before. We might not be able to see him until he's right up close."

Elizabeth suddenly sat up straight on the bed. *"Jessica, what if he can't find us?"*

"Oh, I wouldn't worry about Dad missing the boat," Jessica assured her. "Mom turned on a super-bright yellow light that he could see miles away. This thing is better than the high school's new stadium lights. Dad *can't* miss us."

"Good," Elizabeth said. But Jessica noticed that she shuddered. Too late, Jessica remembered the brilliant lights of the coast-guard cutter as it pulled up alongside Marin's sailboat the week before. They must have blinded Elizabeth on the deck, making it harder for her to see the knife Marin had held above her. Mentioning a boat's bright lights had probably not been her smartest move. The last thing Elizabeth needed was to think about John Marin on a boat at night.

"Actually, it was probably the light that fooled me," Jessica said quickly.

"What are you talking about?" Elizabeth asked.

Jessica shrugged. "Nothing, really. It's just that I thought I spotted Dad getting pretty close to us, when I was outside a few minutes ago."

Elizabeth gasped. "What did you see?"

"For a second I thought I saw a kind of goldish blur," Jessica said. "I figured it was the dinghy, but I was wrong. It disappeared, so I thought I imagined the whole thing. I bet it was a reflection of that bright yellow light on the waves."

Both twins jumped at the sound of a hollow thump. "Dad?" they asked each other in the same breath.

"It sounded like something bumping against the side of the boat," Jessica said, jumping to her feet. "Maybe it was the dinghy!"

Elizabeth shook her head slowly. "No. It

couldn't have been Dad. That noise came from starboard. Dad will be coming from the port side."

"Maybe not!" Jessica jumped to the opposite side of the cabin, where another porthole was set into the wall, between the upper and lower berths of a set of bunk beds. "It's rough out there. What if he got turned around?"

"I don't know," Elizabeth said. "Do you see anything?"

Jessica peered out the porthole. "No," she finally admitted.

The twins' mother appeared in the doorway of the cabin. "That noise was nothing, girls," she said. "The storm must have knocked tree branches and other debris into the water. I guess a stray piece of flotsam thumped against the hull as it floated by."

"You checked for the dinghy?" Elizabeth asked.

"Yes, I looked," their mother said. "It wasn't him."

"What if we're looking on the wrong side of the boat," Jessica suggested, "and he can't yell loud enough for us to hear him?"

"I looked over both sides," her mother assured her. "And there's no dinghy out there. Don't worry, I'm sure your father will be back soon."

Mrs. Wakefield spoke lightly, but Jessica saw tension in her mother's face.

"I'm sure he will be," Elizabeth echoed. Jessica knew that her not-very-convincing smile was for their mother's benefit. A moment later the smile

188

turned into a grimace when a particularly loud gust of wind lashed the side of the boat, drowning out the various creaks, groans, and thwacks that made up the now-familiar background noise of the houseboat in rough water. Jessica fell against her sister, and their mother gripped the door frame for balance.

For a moment Jessica thought she heard an angry voice in the wind. The hair rose on the back of her neck, and she shivered. Then she shook her head, and the voice was gone. The wind was noisy—full of the sounds of moorings that vibrated like guitar strings, of floorboards that creaked and moaned, and of waves whipped to a frenzy. But it was only wind. Gradually, the boat righted itself. Jessica pulled the blanket closer around her bare shoulders.

"I have some more work to do on the deck," Mrs. Wakefield said after she'd regained her balance.

Jessica and Elizabeth dutifully rose to join her.

"No," their mother objected. "Don't even think of helping me, either of you. Besides, I'm almost finished."

"But, Mom—" Jessica began.

"Absolutely not," Mrs. Wakefield insisted. "I want you both to stay here in the cabin until your father returns and to stay warm. You've been chilled through."

"Someone should be out there watching for Dad," Elizabeth pointed out.

"Don't worry. I'll be able to keep an eye out for your father. I promise I'll yell for you as soon as I see him rowing up."

Both twins sighed heavily after their mother disappeared outside.

"I hate boats," Elizabeth said suddenly, flopping back down onto the wide bunk.

Jessica collapsed beside her. "No, you don't. You love boats."

"That was before last Saturday night," Elizabeth countered. "And before *this* Saturday night. I think it'll be a long, long time before I want to get near a boat again."

"There's only one problem with that," Jessica said, a small smile playing on her lips.

"What?" Elizabeth asked.

"We live in a seaside town with about sixty million boats in it. And we work at a marina."

Elizabeth laughed grimly. "OK, so I'm overreacting," she admitted. "But don't invite me on any moonlit sails anytime soon."

"I'm with you on that one," Jessica said. "Next Saturday night let's go bowling instead."

Elizabeth's eyes opened wide with surprise. "You hate bowling. You said it's boring."

Jessica shrugged. "I could do boring," she said.

A wave splashed over the outboard motor and spurted in Mr. Wakefield's face. He tasted salt but continued trying to pry the plastic casing from the motor. He had to get the boat running quickly; nearly a foot of water now sloshed around his calves. It was hard to see anything in the inky darkness, but the motorboat was riding so low in the water that the twins' father knew it was close to sinking. He had already tried the bilge pump, but Marin had damaged it beyond repair.

"This is hopeless!" he exclaimed aloud. "I'll never get this motor fixed before the water rises. I need more time!"

He kicked impatiently, sending a wave of icy water sloshing down the length of the boat. But his foot struck something softer than the boat's wooden floor. He shone the flashlight through the water at his feet and saw the gray canvas cover that had sheltered the front part of the boat from the rain, lying in a water-covered heap. He remembered that he'd tossed it there earlier.

Wait a minute, Mr. Wakefield thought with growing excitement. *That canvas is water-repellent. It might be exactly what I need.*

He knelt in the bilgewater, groping with numb fingers at the bottom of the boat. He had to find the hole through which the sea was slowly but surely seeping.

Marin had done his work well. The jagged gash in the wooden hull was about four inches long and less than two inches wide. A carefully wielded ax blade could have carved it, Mr. Wakefield guessed. He lifted the boat cover from the bilgewater and shook it out. He folded the canvas quickly, arranging a section that looked about the right size, and shoved it into the gash in the hull. He worked the canvas farther into the hole until he thought it would stay put for a while.

Unfortunately, it was only a makeshift solution. Some water was still seeping in around the canvas plug. In fact, he realized with dismay, the hole was actually getting bigger. The boat was old, and the boards were rotting. Marin's ax had done more than tear a gash. It had split the wood of one board, and the split was growing.

The twins' father shook his head. He couldn't worry about that now. For the moment he had managed to slow the leak. If a huge piece of the hull split open later—well, he would worry about that when it happened.

Now I have to bail out enough to keep this thing afloat, he thought. *Then I'll fix the motor and catch up to Marin.*

As he began to bail, he shook his head in wonder at Marin's careful, methodical planning. The murderer had worked out this whole, complicated scheme, right on the spot, as soon as he realized the Wakefields were escaping the island by boat.

As usual, Marin had every detail covered. The hole in the hull was large enough to ensure the boat's demise, but small enough to sink it slowly. The time lapse would have been absolutely necessary for Marin's purposes, Mr. Wakefield realized.

The slow leak gave the twins' father enough time to reach the motorboat before it went under—and had given him enough time to understand fully the fate that Marin had planned for him and his family.

Mr. Wakefield had stumbled right into Marin's trap.

John Marin submerged quickly beneath the chilling waves, holding tight to the houseboat's taut, sinewy anchor line. A surge of water had thrown him hard against the starboard hull of the houseboat. Had anyone heard him?

For a moment he had the impression of movement above him, and a glint of gold. Then it was gone. Marin relaxed and rose back to the water's agitated surface. The gold glimmer was a blond head. Mrs. Wakefield or one of the twins had looked over the side for the source of the thump, had seen nothing, and had gone away. No doubt the three assumed he was a stray tree branch or a forgotten tire, bumping harmlessly against the hull.

Marin peered into the distance one last time. Good. The fog still shrouded the dinghy, which he'd anchored thirty yards away. Its only inhabitants now were Mrs. Clayton's fire ax and Ned's life preserver. Marin was sure he could find the small raft again when the time was right. He might have a long way to swim in order to reach it, but he was a strong swimmer. He knew he could make it. For now, the important thing about the dinghy was to keep it out of sight. Unexpected guests were always the most fun.

For a moment Marin longed for the ax. It was such a powerful weapon; he felt so masterful when his fingers caressed its smooth wooden handle and his arms weighed its substantial heft. But it couldn't be helped. The ax was too big and heavy to carry as he swam from the anchored dinghy to the anchored houseboat. Besides, the ax was a massive, sloppy weapon. He had something cleaner and flashier in mind for the Wakefield women. Through his wet shirt, he felt for his knife. It was still there, hanging from his belt loop on a piece of mooring.

Everything was ready for the final stage of Operation Wakefield.

Carefully, Marin braced his feet against the side of the boat and began pulling himself up the anchor line, walking his feet up the hull while carefully holding his body steady. He couldn't move in utter silence, under the circumstances. But that shouldn't matter. The creaking of the boat and the pounding of the waves against its hull would cover any slight noise he made. He just had to take care not to be too loud.

Suddenly a powerful gust of wind slammed into Marin's body, hurling him against the houseboat's slick hull. His hands burned on the anchor rope as he slid a couple feet down the line. "Oh, hell!" he shouted.

He stopped with a sharp jerk, swinging from the rope. He clamped his jaw shut while he regained his balance. He counted in his head as he listened. *One thousand one . . . One thousand two . . .*

No, he decided after two minutes—they hadn't heard him. The wind and the subsequent pitching of the houseboat had made enough noise to cover the sounds of his near fall and careless exclamation.

Marin breathed deeply for a moment. Then, stealthily, he made his way, hand over hand, to the top of the anchor rope. He pulled himself over the brass railing that surrounded the deck. Then he dropped to the polished planks of the deck, ducking low to remain out of sight.

Somebody else was on the deck, with her back to Marin. She was kneeling a few yards away from him, over some sort of compartment in the floor. Luckily, a bright yellow light that hung between them was pointed in her direction, illuminating Alice Wakefield's golden hair like a halo. It also lit the deck beyond her and reflected off an arc of iridescent black waves on the other side of the ship's far railing. Marin, crouching near the opposite railing, behind the yellow light, was in almost total darkness. He knew that nobody in the lighted circle would be able to see him.

He gazed for a minute at the supple curve of Mrs. Wakefield's back and the grace of her movements, even on an unstable boat. Then he smiled, anticipating his revenge on Ned Wakefield, once and for all.

Mr. Wakefield willed his tired body to bend and straighten, lift and throw. He bailed water from the motorboat faster than he would have thought possible. *It must be between eleven thirty and midnight,* he thought. But he kept bailing. He couldn't take the time to grope around for the flashlight and shine it on his watch. But he guessed that the killer must have had enough time to reach the houseboat by now.

Panic washed over Mr. Wakefield. He stopped bailing. He grabbed the binoculars from the front seat and peered into the night. A sudden gust of wind nearly knocked him off his feet. But when he regained his balance, he saw that the wind had cleared away some of the mist.

He could see the houseboat, its yellow light shining like a star against a black background of water and sky. But where was Marin? The dinghy should be visible too, as a tawny blur somewhere between the motorboat and the houseboat. He scanned the area again, but the lifeboat wasn't there. Part of his mind told him he should be happy not to see the killer closing in on his family. But Mr. Wakefield felt only terror.

I'd rather be able to see him, even watch him row closer to the houseboat, he told himself quietly. *At least then I'd know what he was up to. There's nothing as bad as not knowing.*

Mr. Wakefield turned back to the motor and yanked off the plastic casing with one tug. He had to get the motor running. Now.

The twins' mother shielded her eyes from the houseboat's bright light and peered into the gloom. Her lips were chapped by the strong wind, and she could taste salt on them.

For the hundredth time that night, she wished for a pair of binoculars. *Heck, I'd take a telescope,* she thought. *A periscope. Or even a microscope. I could use it to examine my own sanity. Why in the world did I let Ned go out there by himself?*

Not only was there no sign of her husband's dinghy, but she couldn't even see the motorboat anymore. The fog was too thick, or the boat had drifted too far away. Or the motorboat had capsized.

Mrs. Wakefield felt tears of fear and frustration gathering in her eyes. She didn't want the twins to know it, but she was growing more afraid with every passing second.

She squinted at her watch. It was nearly midnight.

"That's it," she decided aloud. "I can't take this anymore. I don't care about keeping the frequency open for emergencies. This *is* an emergency. I'm calling the coast guard."

＊　　　　＊　　　　＊

Marin stood silently in the shadows, watching Mrs. Wakefield walk resolutely across the deck to the radio. He'd be damned if he was going to allow her to reach it.

Marin whipped a knife from his pocket, admiring its clean, elegant blade of gleaming metal. He raised it carefully, took aim, and deftly sliced through the line that connected the houseboat to its anchor.

The boat jumped free, at the mercy of the wind and waves. And Elizabeth, Jessica, and their mother were at the mercy of John Marin.

The twins' mother felt the boat lurch under her as she reached for the radio transmitter. Suddenly the vessel seemed untamed and dangerously unsteady.

"That's odd," she said aloud. "It feels as if we're adrift."

Mrs. Wakefield grabbed a post for balance and laid her hand on the radio.

Something rammed against the back of her head. The deck tilted up crazily to meet her crumpling body. An instant later, everything went black.

Mr. Wakefield sat at the wheel of the motorboat, the wind whipping his face over the low windshield. He felt as if he were willing the creaking old craft along, rather than driving it. By midnight he had poured so much effort into the motorboat that it seemed like an extension of his own body.

Unfortunately, the boat was as weary and stressed-out as he was. He'd found the problem with the motor as soon as he'd pried off the casing. A spark-plug wire was missing. No doubt Marin had yanked it free and tossed it overboard into the roiling ocean. It hadn't taken long for Mr. Wakefield to figure out that he could substitute a wire from the smashed radio. But like his plug in the hull, the repair was a makeshift one. The boat ran, but only slowly and haltingly.

Mr. Wakefield had never known that plain old water could be so hard—so substantial. The boat lunged forward in fits, its bow ricocheting off waves that felt like boulders under the hull. And with every bounce the motor chugged and sputtered and threatened to die.

He grabbed the binoculars from the seat next to him to check his course against the houseboat's position. It still hung there in the dark, like a pale white ghost carrying a yellow lantern. It was farther away than he'd hoped. But he was getting closer.

Suddenly the yellow light began to glide forward. Mr. Wakefield rubbed his eyes. *That can't be right,* he thought worriedly.

But it was. Somebody had pulled anchor. The houseboat was floating off into the distance.

Fear coursed through his body. His wife and daughters would never have set off alone like that. They would have waited for his return. Somebody else was in control of the houseboat.

Marin.

A minute later the white blur of the houseboat had disappeared. He could no longer see the bright point of yellow light. The twins' father was completely alone in the dark seascape of wind and water.

Chapter 11

Tears blurred Elizabeth's vision as she looked into the storage compartment at her feet. It was the same compartment where her mother had found the medical supplies. But now it was empty, and half its interior was in shadow.

"I said get inside!" Marin yelled, his knife at Jessica's throat. "Do it, Liz! Or there'll be one dead twin lying on the deck."

Elizabeth nodded, her eyes locked on to Jessica's. She stepped into the rectangular hole, which suddenly reminded her of a tiny coffin. She didn't want to scrunch her body into the dark, cramped space and let him close the door over her. "It's too small," she said, her voice broken with a sob.

"Do it," Marin ordered again. "Sit on the bottom and keep your head down. You'll fit."

He slashed the knife across Jessica's neck, and Elizabeth screamed. But Jessica was all right; Marin had held the knife an inch in front of her. He winked at Elizabeth. "Next time I'll slice her for real."

Elizabeth sat in the storage space with her knees up in front of her. Before she lowered her head, she took one last look at the deck of the boat. In reality, the houseboat was pitching wildly on the waves, like some rodeo animal. But in Elizabeth's memory, the scene would always be preserved like a snapshot in the utter stillness of an instant.

The cold yellow spotlight illuminated half the deck, plunging the rest into utter blackness. Marin stood at center stage, his own inky shadow pooled beneath and behind him on the wood planks. One of his muscular arms crossed Jessica's chest, pinning both her hands at her sides. The other held the knife, poised and ready in front of her throat. In his grasp Jessica looked small and fragile, her eyes wide with fear, tears running down her face.

Worst of all, behind Marin on the deck lay the twins' mother. Her eyes were closed; blood streaked her face. Her body lay still, and Elizabeth couldn't tell if she was breathing.

In the next instant Marin narrowed his eyes at Elizabeth, and she slowly lowered her head to her knees. Then he stepped forward, dragging Jessica with him like a rag doll. With his foot he pushed the compartment's lid over Elizabeth with a snap that echoed in her brain. All light vanished.

Something yellowish rose from the black waves ahead of the motorboat. Mr. Wakefield squinted into the night, but the shifting fog obscured the shape of the floating object. He slowed the boat to a chugging halt but kept the engine running. If he turned the engine off, he wasn't sure he'd be able to start it again. He trained the flashlight on the tawny form. It was the dinghy from the houseboat. The dinghy wasn't adrift; beside it a taut anchor line disappeared into the waves. The little boat was empty.

"Why did he leave it out here?" the twins' father asked aloud. "What was he planning?" He scanned the fog with the binoculars, but the houseboat was nowhere in sight.

He anchored the motorboat and slid down the ladder into the dinghy. His own life jacket was there, as well as a heavy, long-handled ax that looked as if it had been taken from a fire-alarm box. He eyed the ax grimly as he weighed it in his hands. It sickened him to think that he might have to use it on another human being, but Marin's acts barely qualified him for membership in the species. And the ax was the only weapon the counselor had. He took it with him when he climbed back into the still-sputtering motorboat.

Water splashed around his feet, three inches deep on the wooden deck. *That canvas plug must be working itself loose in the hole,* he thought. But he decided not to fix it. He couldn't lose any more time. He had to find the houseboat soon. If he didn't, it wouldn't matter if the motorboat sank and dragged him to the bottom of the ocean with it.

Despite the few minutes it cost him, he tied the dinghy behind the motorboat. If he managed to get the twins and his wife off the houseboat and away from Marin, they would need something to escape in, and the motorboat obviously wasn't going much farther. Then he revved the motor again, and the boat leaped forward with an awkward bound.

This has to be a nightmare. It's the only possible explanation, Jessica thought, watching the hatch close over her sister's head.

Jessica had been sure that she and Elizabeth were safe from Marin, at least temporarily. A few minutes earlier the twins had heard footsteps enter the cabin behind them. They had spun around, expecting to see their mother.

The next few seconds had played out in slow motion. Her sister must have known the truth an instant before Jessica had. Jessica remembered seeing a glass of water fall from Elizabeth's hand to the table near the bunk beds. She remembered water splashing her own bare thighs, near the hem of her cutoffs. And she remembered recoiling in horror at the sight of John Marin standing over them, his hair damp and disheveled. A straight, sharp knife had glittered in his hand.

Now Marin held that same knife cold against the front of Jessica's throat.

Two weeks earlier she would have snuggled deliciously into the powerful arm that was wrapped around her bare midriff. But now its pressure on her skin made her feel dirty.

"How did you get here?" she sobbed. "How did you follow us?"

Marin laughed. "Shut up, darling, and do exactly as I tell you," he sneered.

A cramp seared through Elizabeth's left thigh. She longed to stretch out her legs. But the toes of her sneakers were already butting against the opposite wall of the tiny compartment. Stretching was out of the question. She couldn't even massage the cramp away through her shorts; there was no way to get her hand anywhere near her thigh.

Crammed into the small space, Elizabeth had no room to move her legs, her shoulders, or even her head, which rested on her knees in front of her. Her arms, stretched around her knees, had a little more freedom, but not much. She could move them up and down, but not from side to side. As the runaway boat bounced on the waves, she was continually bumped against one side or the other. She was sure she'd have purple bruises on both arms by morning.

If I live until morning, she thought in despair.

The tight fit wouldn't have bothered her nearly as much if it hadn't been for the total darkness in the compartment. Logically, she knew she was alone. The creepy-crawly feelings that kept skating up her bare arms and legs were the products of her own imagination. *There are no bugs in here!* she reminded herself. She would have a much easier time believing that if she could check it out for herself.

Elizabeth couldn't remember ever being somewhere this dark before. She shifted her head a few inches from side to side but couldn't see even a faintly lit outline of the compartment's lid above her. The seal seemed to be absolutely airtight.

Airtight! The hairs stood up on Elizabeth's arms. "How much air is there in here?" she whispered, horrified. "How long do I have until I use it all up?"

For one panic-stricken moment she was sure she was suffocating. Her lungs felt tight, as if an iron band were squeezing the air from them. Her head spun as she gasped for breath.

No, she realized. She couldn't have used up all the oxygen so quickly. She couldn't give in to her fears, or she'd never think of a way out of this.

Elizabeth forced herself to breathe at a slow, steady pace. Once she felt calmer, she realized that she could hear every word being said on the deck above her.

"You won't get away with this!" Jessica challenged Marin, her voice quavery but resolute. "My father will be back any minute, and then you'll be sorry."

Marin laughed—a long, drawn-out cackle that raised goose bumps on Elizabeth's legs. "Your father, my dear, is out of the picture."

"He is not!" Jessica insisted. "He went to help some people on a motorboat! He's on his way back here now!"

"You Wakefields are so gullible," Marin said in a calm, reasonable voice that would have made him sound charming if he hadn't been saying such terrible things. "I suppose it's genetic. At least that's one defect that won't be passed on to any future generations—after I get through with all of you."

Elizabeth gasped. The sinking motorboat had been a setup. Her father had gone on a wild-goose chase, designed to keep him away from his family so that Marin could move in for the kill.

"By now Dad's figured out that you tricked him," Jessica said desperately. "He's on his way back here in the dinghy."

"The dinghy?" Marin said, obviously amused. "Jessica, darling, how do you think *I* got here? Your father doesn't have the dinghy. And by now he doesn't have the motorboat, either. The boat—and your father—are at the bottom of the ocean."

Elizabeth desperately tried to control her quiet sobs, thinking of her rapidly depleting oxygen supply.

"Ned Wakefield, Counselor to the Fishes," Marin continued. "It has quite a ring to it, doesn't it?"

Elizabeth heard muffled thumps and knew that Jessica was struggling with Marin. "Be careful, Jessica!" she whispered, remembering the strength of Marin's viselike arms from her own struggle with him, on the deck of another boat.

A loud *smack* cut short a scream. "You'll get a lot worse than that if you don't shut your mouth and let me tie you up," Marin threatened, his voice harsh and dangerous.

"What difference does it make?" demanded Jessica. "No matter what I do, you're planning to kill us anyway, aren't you?"

When he spoke again, Marin's voice once more had the controlled, affable tone that had fooled Jessica and Elizabeth into thinking he was a harmless, friendly guy. "Yes, I do plan to kill you." It was the same tone of voice he might have used to say that yes, he did plan to see a movie. Elizabeth shuddered. "The only question is when, and how."

"I don't care when or how," Jessica said defiantly. "If you're going to kill me, you might as well do it now."

208

"No, Jessica!" Elizabeth screamed as loudly as she could.

Jessica hesitated but went on. "I'm not going to cooperate with anything you tell me to do, you scumbag! What do you think of that?"

"What I think is immaterial," Marin said smoothly. "Let's see what your sister thinks, shall we? Perhaps she's willing to die quickly, too, just to satisfy your need to defy me."

"No!" Jessica screamed. "Leave Elizabeth alone! I'll let you tie me up. Do whatever you want to me."

"I thought you'd come around," Marin said with a chuckle.

Elizabeth was terrified, but now she was seething mad, as well. She never could stand by and listen to anyone hurt her sister. How dare he manipulate Jessica by threatening Elizabeth? It was the same sleazy tactic he'd used on Elizabeth earlier, to get her to climb into the storage chamber.

Elizabeth's right hand balled into a fist, and she pounded the floor with it. To her surprise she felt something cold and hard under her hand. Elizabeth groped for it and grimaced. A sharp pain slashed through her finger. She dropped the hard object with a metallic clatter. Immediately, Elizabeth felt blood running down her finger, and wiped it on her sock. Whatever she had touched was sharp. If she had the chance, maybe the object could be used on Marin. Elizabeth felt again for the piece of metal, and this time picked it up safely and turned it in her fingers.

The object was a small knife with a razor for a blade, a scalpel. It must have been among the medical supplies that had been stored in the hold before Mrs. Wakefield had taken them out. With the cold steel in her hand, Elizabeth felt stronger. She'd find a way to hurt Marin with it, she vowed.

If she didn't die of suffocation before he opened the lid.

The motorboat lurched over the dark waves, its patched-together motor sputtering and wheezing. Behind it, the inflatable dinghy bounced from side to side on its slender line. Mr. Wakefield kicked at the four inches of water around his feet and prayed that the little motorboat would keep running—and stay afloat—until he found the houseboat and his family.

He held the binoculars to his eyes and scanned the night. The fog was intermittent now, blowing over the water like ragged specters. Finally he saw what he was looking for—a ghostly form up ahead, too white to be a trick of the fog, with a piercing yellow light over it, beckoning.

But the light was moving quickly away from him; the houseboat was picking up speed. Mr. Wakefield simply wasn't sure if the old motorboat would be able to catch it.

Somebody's hand was on Mrs. Wakefield's arm. Her husband must be home. *Yes, that has to be it,* she thought groggily. Who else would have his hand on her arm? But this wasn't home, she remembered. She was too cold, and her lips tasted salty. Now she knew. She was on a boat, and her husband had gone. Was he back now? She wasn't sure. She couldn't think. Her head felt as if it were full of rocks. She tried to open her eyes, but her eyelids were too heavy.

The hand gripped her arm and jerked it behind her back, hard enough to bring tears to her eyes. *This can't be Ned,* Mrs. Wakefield thought. *My husband would never hurt me.* Somebody was tying her up, using rough, sinewy ropes that pulled too tightly and scratched her skin.

"Don't hurt her!" screamed a voice. It was the voice of one of her daughters, Mrs. Wakefield realized, though she couldn't tell which one. In terror, their voices sounded exactly the same. Her daughters were in trouble.

Mrs. Wakefield wrenched her eyes open, and a light like the sun seared her eyeballs. She snapped them shut and tried again, carefully.

Suddenly the twins' mother knew exactly where she was. She was on the houseboat, with the bright yellow light. And a man she recognized from John Marin's photograph was tying her to the deck. To her left Jessica half sat, half sprawled, fastened

211

tightly with rope to iron rings set into the planking. One side of her face was bruised. In her scanty bikini top and short shorts, she looked particularly helpless and out of place.

"Mom!" Jessica cried.

"Keep quiet, both of you!" Marin commanded.

Mrs. Wakefield turned to Jessica. "Elizabeth?"

"She's OK—" Jessica began.

Relieved, the twins' mother let out the breath she hadn't known she was holding. Marin slapped Jessica across the face.

"Don't you dare slap my daughter!" Mrs. Wakefield shouted.

"She'll get another one—and a lot more—if I hear another word out of either of you," Marin warned.

The twins' mother had never met this man, but she would have known who he was even if she'd never seen his photograph. He was handsome, she supposed. Or he would be, if a more pleasant expression replaced the anger that now hardened the lines of his face. His eyes were midnight-blue—almost black—and his body was powerful and well toned, in an unremarkable outfit of blue jeans and a blue-and-white-plaid shirt that hung open over a white T-shirt. In fact, John Marin *looked* perfectly ordinary, not at all the way she'd imagined a convicted killer would look. But he radiated hatred the way a furnace radiates heat.

For no apparent reason except to test her,

Marin kicked Jessica in the side. Jessica groaned, but her mother could see that she wasn't badly hurt. Mrs. Wakefield clenched her teeth to keep from speaking out. *Where is Elizabeth?* she wanted to scream.

As if in answer to her unasked question, Marin turned to look at Mrs. Wakefield, grinning affably. The ogre who had kicked her daughter in a rage only a moment earlier was now replaced by an attractive young man with an easy smile.

"I suppose you're wondering where your daughter's *better* half is," he said, with an amused glance toward the seething Jessica. "To tell you the truth, I'm afraid I forgot to keep track of the time, like I'd planned. There *might* still be some oxygen in that teeny-tiny little space. Then again, there might not be."

Mrs. Wakefield's eyes widened, and she forgot to be silent. *"Where is Elizabeth?"* she yelled.

Marin strolled across the deck to the storage compartment where the girls' mother had found the boat's medical supplies. To her horror, he lifted his foot and tapped on the lid.

Beside her mother, Jessica struggled to break free of her bonds. "You let her out of there!"

"Please," was all the twins' mother could choke out.

Marin shrugged. "Well, when you put it so politely . . ." With agonizing slowness he lifted the hatch of the storage compartment.

Elizabeth's head bobbed convulsively as she gasped for breath. "I'm OK, Jess," she said as soon as she could speak. Then she caught sight of her mother, and her face filled with relief. "Oh, Mom, you're all right. I was so worried—"

"No talking in the ranks, girls," Marin said, shaking his head as if he were scolding naughty children. "Come on, Elizabeth. It's your turn to get roped. I always wanted to be a rodeo star."

He grabbed Elizabeth's arm and jerked her to a standing position. She winced, and her mother could see that she was in pain.

"Give her a minute," Mrs. Wakefield pleaded. "She's all cramped up from being stuffed into that box."

"I'll be OK in a second," Elizabeth said, still panting. She leaned over for a minute, the way a runner does after a race, and rested her hands on her shins, as if trying to catch her breath. Her mother's eyes widened as Elizabeth whipped a small scalpel from her sock and held it in her palm.

Mrs. Wakefield's eyes were on her daughter's cupped hand as Elizabeth slowly straightened up. Then Elizabeth sprang into action and thrust the knife toward Marin's stomach.

Marin's affable manner vanished. As quick as a panther, he grabbed Elizabeth's wrist and twisted. With a cry of pain she dropped her small, innocuous-looking knife. Marin kicked it away, still gripping her wrist.

"You little idiot," he said into her ear, his voice ugly with hate. "Don't you know by now that you can't get the better of me? Don't you know that I can crush you"—he twisted her wrist farther— "anytime I want to?"

Elizabeth's knees buckled, but Marin jerked her up cruelly.

"Stop it!" Jessica and her mother screamed together.

Marin only laughed. Then he threw Elizabeth to the deck next to her sister and tied her tightly.

"You know, there's something I really regret about all of this," Marin told them as he gave his final knot one last tug.

"How sad for you," Jessica remarked.

Marin just grinned at her and disappeared around the side of the cabin. He returned a moment later with a metal canister of gasoline. Mrs. Wakefield gasped, afraid that she finally knew exactly what Marin had in mind for them.

Marin continued speaking, as if he had never stopped. "The entire point of my whole plan, of course, was to get back at my old friend Ned, in a way that would be sure to get his attention." He began pouring gasoline onto the deck, in a circle around Alice and the twins. Some spattered on Mrs. Wakefield's pants leg, and the smell overpowered the scents of sea and salt that had permeated everything around her until that moment.

"No!" Jessica screamed. "How can you do this?"

"It appears that my plan has succeeded," Marin said smoothly, ignoring the interruption. "What I regret is that I've now got you all exactly where I want you, and poor old Ned isn't even here to see it."

He drained the last of the gasoline can onto Jessica's cutoff jeans. "Denim burns very nicely, you know," he confided to her, still smiling.

"Let my daughters go!" Mrs. Wakefield pleaded. "You can do whatever you like to me."

"Mom!" Jessica screamed.

At the same time, Elizabeth cried, "No!"

Marin disappeared into the cabin. He returned a moment later with a box of wooden matches in his hand. He slipped one out, lit it, and held it over Jessica's head, grinning.

"Untie my daughters," the girls' mother proposed again, trying to keep her voice calm. "You'll still have me here. That's enough revenge on my husband. He'll be devastated. Please."

Marin laughed and blew out the match. "Oh, Alice, you're so beautiful and so earnest. But I forgot—you still believe your husband is alive."

"What are you saying?" Mrs. Wakefield whispered.

"I guess you were a little indisposed earlier," Marin said with mock sadness, "when I was telling Jessica about Ned's watery grave."

Mrs. Wakefield felt blood rushing to her head and shook it so she wouldn't faint. She couldn't let

216

herself believe Marin, not when her daughters were in so much danger.

Marin lit another match and stared into its flame. She saw fire reflected in his midnight-blue eyes, shimmering there like the fragmented reflections of the boat's yellow beacon light in the dark, treacherous waves.

Suddenly Marin shoved the lit match toward Mrs. Wakefield's face. "I do regret that Ned won't be able to watch you all die," he told her. "Oh, well, I'm sure he imagined your deaths many, many times—as the water closed in over his head. Ned had such a marvelous imagination. You know, I think I'm going to miss him."

Jessica's eyes followed Marin's hand as he gestured with another lit match.

"Life is so fragile," he mused, staring at the flame. "One minute you're alive and arguing cases in court, sending people to prison for years. . . ." His eyes hardened, and he looked, one by one, at the twins' mother, at Jessica, and then at Elizabeth, as if reassuring himself that he had their attention. "And the next minute, you're fish food," he concluded. He blew out the flame.

Marin tossed the spent match aside. "Of course, you three will die a little faster than the counselor did," he said, "though I have tried to pour the fuel a couple feet out from you. I wanted to give you a few minutes to really contemplate what's happening to you. It's so much more meaningful that way, don't you think, Alice?"

He pulled another match from the box and lit it. Then he tossed it into a pool of gasoline a few feet from Mrs. Wakefield's back. With a sickening *whoosh,* flame billowed up like a sail behind her.

Elizabeth screamed.

Jessica, tied between Elizabeth and her mother, looked at them both. In their faces she saw reflected her own fear and horror. What she didn't see was the intense anger that was rising in her chest. She had never in her life wanted to kill somebody the way she wanted to kill John Marin at that moment. But the only body parts she had free were her left foot and her right elbow. Neither seemed to be of much use for harming Marin or for freeing herself and the others.

"Alice, I do wish we'd had more time together," Marin said sadly, his face orange in the glow of the fire. From the tone of his voice he could have been toasting marshmallows at Boy Scout camp.

Marin lit another match and gestured toward Elizabeth with it. "Liz, honey, I enjoyed our last sail, even if it was cut short—I'm glad *this* one won't end before I've finished showing you a really hot time." He tossed the match into a shallow puddle of gasoline a few feet away from her, where it burst into flame.

"And Jessica—brash, fun-loving Jessica—I'm sorry I couldn't put you on television sooner. I'm glad I can oblige you now. Too bad you won't be around to watch the news: 'The bodies of three women were found with the charred remains of a houseboat, et cetera, et cetera.'" He laughed. "Good-bye, Jessica. You were truly a fun date."

He pulled out another match, flicked it to life, and began to toss it toward Jessica.

Something barreled into him from one side, and Marin sprawled onto the deck. The lit match, knocked from his hand, fell toward Jessica, but the flame burned out before it brushed harmlessly by her leg.

Marin rolled a few feet. Then he jumped up and disappeared into the shadows outside the circle of light.

A second man was on board, and he was fighting with Marin in the dark. Jessica couldn't see them. "Who is it?" she screamed above the roar of the flames, praying that her mother or sister had got a better look than she had. "Was it Dad?" *It had to be,* she told herself. *Who else could it be?*

"I couldn't tell for sure!" Elizabeth screamed back, her voice hoarse with the smoke. "Jessica, the fire's getting closer to me!"

"Work your hands free, girls!" the twins' mother yelled. "One of mine is coming loose!"

Elizabeth screamed again and then fell into a coughing fit. Jessica could already feel the heat of the flames on her face and legs. The powerful gasoline smell reminded her that her clothes were drenched with the stuff. And the smell of smoke was getting stronger.

Something crashed onto the part of the deck outside the light. Jessica turned her head, but her vision couldn't pierce the darkness. A stray spark caught her attention as it floated through the air toward her. Her eyes followed it, willing it to extinguish itself in midair, as the last match had. The spark landed in the ends of her mother's hair, and a trickle of fire rose from it.

"Mom!" Jessica screamed. She reached out with her free elbow and managed to smother the flame.

Suddenly two male figures staggered into view. Mr. Wakefield swung at Marin with an ax, forcing him close to where Jessica lay tied to the deck. Mrs. Wakefield screamed. Marin, the quicker of the two men, lunged to the side. Then he stepped in to jab his knife toward the counselor's ribs.

"Dad!" Elizabeth coughed.

Jessica acted. As Marin lunged toward her father, she extended her left foot as far as she could. Marin tripped and dropped the knife, sprawling on the deck with a thud. Mr. Wakefield shifted the ax in his hands. He swung the ax in a wide arc and slammed its handle against the side of Marin's head. Marin lay still.

"Ned!" Mrs. Wakefield cried. "Free Elizabeth first!"

Hungry tongues of flame licked at Elizabeth's bare legs. As Jessica watched in horror, a fiery

220

tendril leaped out from the main blaze, igniting Elizabeth's sleeve. Her father sprang to her side and snuffed it out with his hands. As the flames roared around him, he used Marin's knife to cut the ropes holding Elizabeth in place. Then he bounded to his wife and freed her, while Elizabeth untied Jessica's hands.

"This way to the dinghy!" he cried, motioning them away from the flame. "Hurry! The fire has spread to the cabin. The whole boat's going to blow when it reaches the fuel tanks."

Jessica grabbed Elizabeth's hand and sprinted across the deck, following their father. Just behind her, she could hear their mother's ragged breathing. She realized that the wind was tossing the flames around the deck. Everywhere the fire touched, it took hold, igniting the wood all around them. The smoke hung heavy in the air, smelling acrid and making it hard to breathe. The air was hot and gritty on Jessica's bare skin. She felt as if she were running through a tunnel of fire. Behind her, her mother began coughing uncontrollably.

Mr. Wakefield reached the brass railing at the edge of the deck and gestured over it. Jessica looked down and saw the mustard-colored dinghy below, illuminated now in the uneven, flickering light of the fire.

"Quick!" the twins' father yelled. "Grab the rope and slide over the side," he instructed, pushing

221

Elizabeth to a rope tied to a cleat on the railing. The dinghy was directly underneath it. "Jessica, you're next! Be ready to go over the side as soon as I tell you."

"Dad, there's another boat down there!" Jessica shouted.

"It's the motorboat we saw before," Mr. Wakefield explained. "But it's practically submerged. It'll sink completely in another few minutes."

Jessica climbed over the railing and tested the rope in her hands. A crashing roar and a flash of light made her stop. A shower of sparks erupted from the part of the deck where Jessica knew the cabin was, though a wall of flame now blocked her view.

"The boat's electricity just shorted out," Mrs. Wakefield explained between coughs. Firelight shone in her eyes.

Jessica nodded, now understanding why the night suddenly seemed darker, despite the fire's ghastly orange cast. The bright yellow light no longer shone over the deck.

"Ned, how will we make it to shore in that little boat?" Mrs. Wakefield asked, recovering her breath. "We don't even know where we are."

"Don't worry," her husband assured her. "This fire will bring the coast guard here in no time."

Mrs. Wakefield nodded. "Go on down, Jessica!" she said. "Hurry!"

"Alice, you're next," Mr. Wakefield said. "When you reach the dinghy, take it out a safe distance from the houseboat. Wait for me there. I have to go back." He gestured toward the inferno on the other end of the deck.

"Dad!" Jessica wailed.

"Jessica, go!" her father ordered.

"Ned, what are you talking about?" Jessica heard her mother asking from above her head as she shimmied down the rope. "Where are you going?"

His answer was lost to Jessica in the roar of wind, waves, and fire.

Elizabeth felt as if she'd been transported into an old movie she'd once seen about the sinking of the *Titanic.* The cold, rough sea and the black night were the same as in the movie. And the houseboat also looked like something out of a movie; it was too terrible to be real. The boat's surface was a thick carpet of flame. Soot and other debris rained into the waves around her like confetti, with an occasional fragment still burning as it fell.

Jessica was in the dinghy, too, sitting beside Elizabeth near the bow. Their mother was just lowering herself into the stern from the rope that hung from the houseboat's railing.

"Mom! What are you doing?" Elizabeth screamed as Alice cut the line that held the dinghy to the side of the larger boat. "Where's Dad? We can't just leave him behind!"

"Take an oar, Liz," her mother instructed, keeping the other one for herself in the back of the boat. "I don't like it any better than you do, but he's gone back to get Marin. He says he'll jump overboard with him and swim to us."

"*What?*" Jessica yelled. Elizabeth saw fire in her sister's eyes that had nothing to do with the fire on the houseboat. "That's ridiculous!" Jessica continued. "Marin practically killed us all! Why the heck does Dad want to save his nasty, pathetic excuse for a life?"

Elizabeth wouldn't have put it quite so bluntly, but she had to agree.

"Jessica, your father said there's a flashlight up there at the very tip of the bow. Find it and keep it focused ahead of us. Give a yell if you see any debris in the water that we need to steer around."

"But Mom! Dad is—" Jessica began.

"Jessica!" Mrs. Wakefield interrupted sharply. "I know. But there's nothing you can do for him right now. Just do as I said—please."

Jessica nodded glumly.

"Mom, I don't understand," Elizabeth ventured, trying to keep her voice reasonable. "Letting a monster like Marin live is one thing. But Dad risking his life to save him—"

"I wanted to argue with your father," the twins'

224

mother admitted, pumping away at her oar. "But there was no time for—"

An explosion rocked the ocean around them. Elizabeth whirled. As she stared in shock, the houseboat erupted in a fountain of flame and smoke.

Jessica screamed. Elizabeth turned to her sister and gasped, startled. The eerie orange light made Jessica's hair glow as if it were on fire, too.

"It's all right, girls," their mother said, with only a note of panic in her carefully controlled voice. "Your father had plenty of time to get off the boat. I'm sure he's in the water right now, swimming toward us."

"Why did Dad have to go back?" Jessica cried, sobbing. "It doesn't make any sense! He didn't even know if Marin was still there to save. What if Marin had already woken up and jumped off the boat himself? Then Dad would be risking his life, while Marin was already—"

She froze as she realized what she was saying. In her mind Elizabeth completed her sister's thought: *While Marin was already swimming away.* Elizabeth peered around at the dark, choppy waves, each one gilt-edged with the reflected glow of the fire. What if John Marin was under those black waves right now, swimming silently toward the dinghy?

Suddenly a male hand rose from the waves and grasped the side of the boat. Elizabeth screamed.

The nightmare isn't over, she thought in horror. *Marin is back.*

A head bobbed to the surface. "Is everyone all right?" Mr. Wakefield asked.

He was breathing heavily, but he was alive.

Elizabeth, Jessica, and their mother all sprang forward to help pull him into the dinghy. For the next few minutes they all hugged each other, weary but grateful to be together and safe.

Elizabeth wasn't sure she wanted to hear the answer to her next question, but she knew she had to ask it. She raised her head from where it rested against her father's wet shoulder. "Dad, what about Marin? Did he escape from the boat before you got to him?"

Mr. Wakefield shook his head. "Marin is dead."

Jessica's face showed disbelief, and Elizabeth was sure that her own held exactly the same expression.

"Are you sure, Dad?" Jessica asked. "Are you absolutely sure he's dead?"

"He's dead, all right," their father told them. "I saw the body. The smoke got to him before I could."

"Thank heaven he's the only casualty," Mrs. Wakefield said. "Thank heaven." She was sobbing, and her husband wrapped his arms around her.

Jessica was crying, too, a reflection of orange flames glinting in each tear as it rolled down her face. Elizabeth was startled to realize that her own face was wet with tears, but she wasn't sure if they were tears of fear or relief.

"We made it," Elizabeth whispered, patting her sister's arm. "We're finally safe."

Then she straightened her back, dipped her oar into the water, and resolved to put the burning boat far behind her.

Bantam Books in the Sweet Valley High series
Ask your bookseller for the books you have missed

SIGN UP FOR THE SWEET VALLEY HIGH® FAN CLUB!

Hey, girls! Get all the gossip on Sweet Valley High's® most popular teenagers when you join our fantastic Fan Club! As a member, you'll get all of this really cool stuff:

- Membership Card with your own personal Fan Club ID number
- A Sweet Valley High® Secret Treasure Box
- Sweet Valley High® Stationery
- Official Fan Club Pencil (for secret note writing!)
- Three Bookmarks
- A "Members Only" Door Hanger
- Two Skeins of J. & P. Coats® Embroidery Floss with flower barrette instruction leaflet
- Two editions of *The Oracle* newsletter
- Plus exclusive Sweet Valley High® product offers, special savings, contests, and much more!

Be the first to find out what Jessica & Elizabeth Wakefield are up to by joining the Sweet Valley High® Fan Club for the one-year membership fee of only $6.25 each for U.S. residents, $8.25 for Canadian residents (U.S. currency). Includes shipping & handling.

Send a check or money order (do not send cash) made payable to "Sweet Valley High® Fan Club" along with this form to:

SWEET VALLEY HIGH® FAN CLUB, BOX 3919-B, SCHAUMBURG, IL 60168-3919

NAME_____
           (Please print clearly)

ADDRESS_____

CITY_____ STATE_____ ZIP_____
                                              (Required)

AGE_____ BIRTHDAY_____ /_____ /_____

Offer good while supplies last. Allow 6-8 weeks after check clearance for delivery. Addresses without ZIP codes cannot be honored. Offer good in USA & Canada only. Void where prohibited by law.
©1993 by Francine Pascal   LCI-1383-123

Life after high school gets even *Sweeter!*

Jessica and Elizabeth are now freshmen at Sweet Valley University, where the motto is: Welcome to college — welcome to freedom!

Don't miss any of the books in this fabulous new series.

♥ College Girls #1   0-553-56308-4 $3.50/$4.50 Can.
♥ Love, Lies and   0-553-56306-8
   Jessica Wakefield #2 $3.50/$4.50 Can.
♥ What Your Parents   0-553-56307-6
   Don't Know #3 $3.50/$4.50 Can.
♥ Anything for Love #4   0-553-56311-4 $3.50/$4.50 Can.
♥ A Married Woman #5   0-553-56309-2 $3.50/$4.50 Can.
♥ The Love of Her Life #6   0-553-56310-6 $3.50/$4.50 Can.

- -

Bantam Doubleday Dell
Books for Young Readers

Bantam Doubleday Dell
Dept. SVU 12
2451 South Wolf Road
Des Plaines, IL 60018

Please send the items I have checked above. I am enclosing $_____ (please add $2.50 to cover postage and handling). Send check or money order, no cash or C.O.D.s please.

Name _____

Address _____

City _____ State _____ Zip _____

Please allow four to six weeks for delivery.
Prices and availability subject to change without notice.   SVU 12 4/94

Your friends at Sweet Valley High have had their world turned upside down!

Meet one person with a power so evil, so dangerous, that it could destroy the entire world of Sweet Valley!

A Night to Remember, the book that starts it all, is followed by a six book series filled with romance, drama and suspense.

♡ 29309-5 A NIGHT TO REMEMBER (Magna Edition) ..$3.99/4.99 Can.
♡ 29852-6 THE MORNING AFTER #95...........................$3.50/4.50 Can.
♡ 29853-4 THE ARREST #96..$3.50/4.50 Can.
♡ 29854-2 THE VERDICT #97 ....$3.50/4.50 Can.
♡ 29855-0 THE WEDDING #98...$3.50/4.50 Can.
♡ 29856-9 BEWARE THE BABYSITTER #99.....................$3.50/4.50 Can.
♡ 29857-7 THE EVIL TWIN #100 ....$3.99/4.99 Can.

- -

Bantam Doubleday Dell
Books for Young Readers

Bantam Doubleday Dell
BFYR 20
2451 South Wolf Road
Des Plaines, IL 60018

Please send the items I have checked above. I am enclosing
$_____ (please add $2.50 to cover postage and handling).
Send check or money order, no cash or C.O.D.s please.

_____
Name

_____
Address

_____
City   State   Zip

BFYR 20 1/94

Please allow four to six weeks for delivery.
Prices and availability subject to change without notice.

*Songs from
the Hit TV Series*

Featuring:

*"Rose Colored
Glasses"*

"Lotion"

*"Sweet Valley High
Theme"*

SABAN
RECORDS ™

*Available on CD and Cassette
Wherever Music is Sold.*

™, & © 1995 Saban. All Rights Reserved. SWEET VALLEY HIGH is a trademark of Francine Pascal and is used under license.